A fist crashed on Blue's soldier, a fist carrying a knife. The blade cut through his shirt and scraped across his hip. Blue hit the floor and kicked out backward at what had come at him.

His hip burned, and his arm was numb. He rolled fast, conscious only that he needed a weapon. He didn't know what he was fighting. He needed to wipe his eyes clear and get ready.

"You righteous son of a bitch," Buckminster snarled.

Then Blue was picked up and shaken, and slammed into the wall. He kicked out and heard the gasp and tasted the foul breath in his face. The big man held him in midair and laughed, and two big hands wrapped around Blue's throat.

No light, no air; his heart raced and then slowed. Blue hung from Buckminster's hands and began to die slowly. . . .

Also by William A. Luckey:

THE DEATH OF JOE GILEAD
LONG RIDE TO NOWHERE
BAD COMPANY*

*Published by Fawcett Books

CIMARRON BLOOD

William A. Luckey

FAWCETT GOLD MEDAL • NEW YORK

A Fawcett Gold Medal Book
Published by Ballantine Books
Copyright © 1992 by William A. Luckey

Library of Congress Catalog Card Number: 91-92404

ISBN 0-449-14806-8

Manufactured in the United States of America

First Edition: July 1992

12 11 10 9 8 7 6 5 4 3

for Willow Grace

PART ONE

ONE

His TIME COULD be measured in broken bones or bullet holes, he decided. He rubbed his thigh muscle gingerly, avoiding the tender hole ringed with new pink flesh. Broken bones and bullet holes—hell of a way for a man to mark a short life.

The bay gelding Blue Mitchell rode snorted and sidestepped and only reluctantly answered the pressure of the rider's leg to walk back on the trail. The packhorse, loaded lightly with a few supplies, paid no attention to the bay's foolishness. Blue applauded the brown's common sense.

Right now, at this moment, any man could question Blue's good sense. Headed north in midwinter, up from doubtful warmth of the high New Mexico desert, toward the wide plains edged by cold mountains. In another day's traveling he'd need the warmth of the clumsy sheepskin coat tied high behind his old saddle. Blue shook his head; he didn't think much of riding into the cold, but a man rode where the jobs were, and this time the job meant heading north until he crossed the waters of the Cimarron River.

The bay ducked his head and bucked, more of a crow-hop, but the action angered Blue. He drew up the reins, touched the bay with his spurs, and clamped down on a rising temper. Hell, the bay felt good, that's all. Liked the trail underfoot, liked getting out and moving again, after waiting until Blue's bullet-punched leg healed over. Shot in anger;

3

hell, he'd been more than shot trying to sort life out for another man up on a dry mesa. Dragged and chased and then shot. Not again; this time it would be different. Blue snorted, sounding much like the nervy bay. Then he laughed when the bay threw his head back. This time had better be different.

Blooded stock, the man said, then read out the names writ down on paper, fancy names and numbers. Good horses, left too long and needing the hand of a good man to tame them. Never said the word break, never asked Blue to kill their spirit; instead, the new boss put hard meaning to saying he thought highly of his horses and wanted them tamed and rideable, but not broken.

At first Blue thought to say no to the man, a little runt with a big mouth talking at him, a grim face and nervous hands that wiped together in continuous motion. Blue'd touched his sore leg just then, and the flaring reminder spoke of all the trouble he'd just gotten out of, all for bragging to ride down an outlaw horse. But the proud old man who stood in front of Blue and laid out his needs wouldn't quit. He rubbed his hands and spoke a price that caught Blue's attention, talked of the grasslands and the shaded river run through the ranchhouse ground. Even talked on ducks and geese and elk and sometimes bear that come down to the river to drink. Orchards full of fruit trees, a town with a fine hotel. And hard cash at the end of the deal, and no other boss to tell him how to work the stock.

It was a deal right hard to refuse. Eight horses, the old man said. His hands stopped moving for a bit; eight horses, mostly thoroughbreds, though there was a team of part-Morgans needed work. And a big coming four year old, uncut and real fancy. The old man's hands started kneading each other then, and Blue cursed himself for not paying attention. A superb colt, a future herd sire, if Blue could put manners on him. The old man coughed and swallowed hard. No good keeping a horse entire if he could not be taught manners and obedience. Then the old man apologized for not having the colt started earlier, last winter. Said some-

4

thing about his wife dying and his mind not being on the business at hand.

Blue shied from the implications of people and more demands, and the old man was quick, sharp, for he saw the flinch Blue tried to stop, and he put out a hand, let it rest on Blue's arm. The light blue eyes sought out contact with Blue, the face stilled, the hands quieted. "Son, there won't be people you have to deal with. There's only me and my daughter at the ranch, and our hands. You will have your own house; you can work by yourself. You don't need to be part of our daily lives at all. You need only work with the horses. Does that suit you more?"

As if the old man saw into Blue's frayed soul and dug out the fear in him, the softness bled dry by men who promised friendship, the gentle streak wounded by pretty girls and tired mothers.

The old man's insightful promise took away the last of Blue's reluctance, and he stuck out his hand, renamed the price, and the old man wagged his head in great pleasure, all the while pumping Blue's hand up and down.

Blue set his mind to the old man as he talked horses. He glanced out as the new boss gestured with pride to the chestnut mare tied to the railing in front of the adobe building. Blue stared at the mare, counting up her faults, and decided he had for once made a good choice. If that mare was any comment on the stock he hired on to ride, Blue felt he would be getting paid for having fun. He shivered and wiped down his long face. Next to getting into trouble, horses were what he did best.

He listened to the old man's voice, Martin Smith, he said to call him, in the middle of a bragging sentence, and sat back to think and worry. There wasn't much else Blue could do to make a living; even with the game leg from the bullet he could still ride. But not much else. He wasn't good at throwing a loop over a running steer, and he didn't take to riding those long lines of barbed fence. And he sure as hell didn't think kindly on living in a town, clerking behind a store counter to make daily wage. He had his dreams, lots

5

of them, mostly about raising his own good horses, maybe even a wife and kids. But not now, not yet, not while he could still ride the rankest bucking horse and get a snorty bronc to walk slow and carry a passenger—do a job.

Blue shook his head and got up real quick, and the old man kept talking while watching Blue most careful. That old one was crafty, clever. Blue wondered how the rancher had found him in the Santa Fe saloon, midday and late February. The old man suddenly shut his mouth and stood, backed away from Blue, and the bright eyes narrowed, the flapping mouth got tight. Blue recognized the signs and got real quiet, real ready for what might come next.

He had a suspicion old Martin Smith hadn't really looked Blue straight on and solid when he first came in talking to him. Blue held out his hand right then, in no hurry but wanting to seal the bargain. He gave Smith time, used to the peculiarities of mankind, especially in reference to his own peculiar self.

It was his face and eyes, he knew that now. Heard enough ladies tell him, watched enough men shake their heads and offer to fight after sighting on him. It was the eyes, strange to the rest of the world, but they saw what he needed and laughed when he chose. Ocean color, one man told him, like the middle of winter in pale sunlight. Didn't sound too interesting to Blue, but then he wasn't much on such quarreling. Ocean eyes, set in bright white, set deep in his head and arrogant to match his temper.

Blue shrugged and tried to look at Smith without staring, giving the man his room to make judgments. It was the odd eyes and the bony face, the long body and the big, awkward hands. The blond hair grew too fast, and he forgot about it, tied it back with rawhide. Hair streaked by sunlight, rope thick and always in his face. Hands long and heavy, long-legged and no hipped; not much of a figure but good on a horse, good enough to rope and settle a bronc, good enough to ride out the high bucking and ease the wild spirit without killing it.

He'd learned this much in his supposed twenty-three years

of life on earth; he was hell on friendships and women and damned good with a horse. So he let Martin Smith take an extra long look, study him with reasonable care, and then accept Blue's hand to seal the agreement.

Here he was again, sore and half-healed and willing to ride north in midwinter to take the sting out of good-blooded stock. Tasting fresh air and excitement about a new place. Goddamn, but he needed a guardian.

That had been a week past; now Blue felt the quick bite of the blowing wind, and he hunched deeper in the saddle and shook slightly from the teasing air. The bay gelding half bucked again, head high, ears pricked toward the distant mountains. Blue laughed and slapped the bay neck. He deserved an easy ride and good times in a new place. Blue eased the reins, put spurs to the bay, and let the horse run out a burst of energy. The brown, demoted to packhorse, laid back its ears in displeasure and pulled hard on the lead.

The country changed quickly, intriguing Blue. The miles of narrow hills and deep gullies sided by piñon and juniper were gone now. Ahead lay high grass and sloping hillocks, turrets of gleaming rock, and the ever-present haze of the great mountains. Deep ruts marked man's passage and tripped the quick-footed bay until Blue reined the two horses in and continued at a walk. The tracks were from the old, high-wheeled carts, carrying goods from Kansas into New Mexico and beyond. Tracks rarely used, now that railroads crossed the land, carrying items of ladies' fashions and gents' importance.

Blue grinned at himself; already getting set in his ways, already talking "old" before his time. He was only twenty-three and missed the old times, when a man depended on himself and his horse, his rifle and knife, not on the city law or the smooth track of a built road. He laughed louder, getting old at twenty-three.

He held to the track until it veered east. Smith told him to ride north along the mountains until he came to the Cimarron, so he guided the two horses through the lush grass and the deep gullies, splashed through the cold streams, and began to hunger for a hot meal, a sound other than the bay's snorting and the noise of his own breathing.

He was getting too used to people; he was losing his independence. He had a quick notion to ride on, up into the belly of the hard mountains, and not make it to Martin Smith's ranch. But he'd given his word, shook hands; Martin Smith owned his time until the horses were broke and willing. The notion disappeared, Blue cocked his head and dreamed he heard a voice calling to him.

The bay must have heard the same voice, for the horse shied badly, then took advantage of the loosened rein to bog his head and let out a series of determined bucks. Blue grabbed horn, embarrassed at what he was doing and angry at the bay for making him do it. The bay broke wind and hit the rocky ground with stilted legs, and Blue groaned out loud at the ache in his leg. Then he caught the rein, drew the bay head up with harsh jerks, and goaded the horse into running flat out with the edge of his spurs.

The ground went from rock to grass, and the bay lowered his quarters and put his heart into running. The lead rope to the more cautious brown burned through Blue's hand, and he let go, as eager now as the bay to hit full speed.

The words were not clear, but their sound brought Blue's head up. A man on a laboring paint raced beside him, his dark face clearly grinning. The man rode so close, Blue thought he could count the white teeth bared at him. The words made no sense, but the gestures were inviting him to a race. Blue nodded once and tapped the bay on the shoulder, touched the sweaty sides, and the horse leapt as if the paint beside him had quit running. Blue threw back his head and felt his hat blow off to tug at the end of the rawhide thongs. Strands of bright hair swished past his eyes, and he howled in delight.

There were four men mounted on dancing horses close to an embankment. A man rode off to his right, spurring and whipping the failing paint as if to catch up with the bay. Fear jumped inside Blue as he made out the scowling features of the waiting men. He began to slow the bay until one man, on a proud cream horse, raised an arm in salute and insulted the laboring paint. Laughter rose from the bunched riders, and Blue rode on instinct, lying over the bay's neck and letting the horse run full out.

When he crossed a line near the embankment, he drew up the bay in a small circle. The riders came toward him now, slowly, holding in their horses yet using spurs until the animals pranced and half reared from the conflicting signals. The men rode erect, proudly. Their faces showed only pleasure and delight at the speed of the now-tired bay.

It was a full two minutes before the still-racing paint caught up to the group. Blue heard the rise of laughter and jeering and hoped that the losing rider would not take out his humiliation on Blue's hide. He patted the bay, more to comfort himself than to soothe the horse, which stood quietly, ribs heaving from the race, one hind foot cocked in evident relaxation. Blue cursed his foolishness; if these men had any idea of stealing from him, he had no horse left to get away.

The tall man on the cream stopped a few feet from Blue and removed his hat in a wide bow, offering a quick spewing of unknown words in some kind of tribute. Blue cocked his head, knowing enough of the language to hear the praise but not fully understand the offer. A new rider brought up the steady brown as the leader of the small band expanded his offer.

Blue still did not understand what was being laid out for him; his heart still raced from the effort of the run and his instinctive distrust of the men. But the leader spoke freely, hands waving toward the reviving bay, mouth wide and quick with the half-comprehended words.

Then a headstall and bit of some great value were raised in front of Blue's eyes, and a braided quirt, a small leather pouch, which rang out a silver sound. He was being offered a fine sum for the evident speed of the bay gelding. Blue settled in his saddle, wiped his wet face, and then laid his hand along his thigh. He shook his head slowly, forced a long, sad look on his homely face, and pointed at the mo-

9

tionless brown, pointed again at the supplies strapped to the packsaddle.

There were no more words passed between the group of men and Blue; a man quickly dismounted from a sturdy sorrel and stripped off the gaudy saddle, an inlaid bridle. A halter and rope were fastened to the broad head, and a blanket was left on the wide back. The lead was presented to Blue, and the man on the cream grinned even wider and finally said, in understandable English, "Señor, now you can have no reason to refuse my offer. Your bay is too much to be a good cow pony; he is destined to be a racer, and I would own him and his speed. Your packhorse is far too fine to be carrying such a burden; it is for the likes of this sorrel to be the servant and for you to be mounted on the good brown, who will wear the braided headstall and carry the silver bit in observance of his master's pride and great skill."

The words were flowery and sly, yet the humor dulled their bite and allowed Blue to respond in kind. He held out his hand, and the headstall was almost gently laid across his palm. The weight of the braided horsehair and bit was surprising; Blue dropped his own reins on the bay's neck and fingered the intricately carved cheek pieces of the metal, staring in awe at the curved spoon and inlaid stones, which turned the bit into a work of art. The headstall itself was deeply patterned, woven from many different colors of horse hair. The entire outfit was way past the means of an ordinary vaquero.

Blue looked directly into the dark eyes of the man on the cream gelding. He spoke slowly, as his efforts in the Spanish tongue were awkward and childish. He did not wish to make a costly mistake. The rider raised a hand and interrupted. "Señor, I am called Ruben Martinez. It is enough you will try to speak our tongue; we will not be insulted if you use your own. For we can speak easily in either language. Señor, it is most important that there are no mistakes in our conversation, for we are dealing here with important matters."

The man laughed then. His cream horse half reared and turned, and Blue saw that it was a stallion the big man rode.

The hands of the man barely moved, yet the cream stallion came back to ground and sidestepped until Blue could feel the heat of the horse's body and smell the fine leather of the carved saddle and woolen blanket.

"Señor, it is a fine horse you ride, who can outrun the good paint of my amigo. It is a fine bay that I would offer to trade with you, a sorrel pack animal, so you may once again ride the brown, and a headstall of which you can be proud, a bit to control the brown's every move, and a few coins to ring in your pocket. Now, Señor, I cannot be more fair than this."

Blue hung the headstall from his saddle horn and stuck out his hand. "Señor, it is a deal."

The man's smile grew bigger, and his companions whirled their horses in celebration. "Then it is settled, and you will come with us now if you wish. We will offer you good food and drink, a night among new friends, a chance to rest on your long trip to the hacienda of Señor Martin Smith."

It was a game they played, and Blue saw the rules laid out for him. His job was already known, his progress marked by curious riders, his handling of the hot bay noted and admired. Old habit made him stare a moment too long into the big man's eyes, as if to seek out any hidden lie, dig into any act of betrayal. The big man on the obedient cream stallion looked back into Blue's eyes and did not back down, nor did he offer a challenge or find an insult in Blue's behavior.

As if an understanding was drawn between the two men, they extended their hands at the same time, to shake on a horse trade and perhaps a moment of friendship. The brown's burden was packed on the sorrel, and Blue's gear was stripped from the bay and placed on the brown's back. The brown fussed at accepting the heavy silver bit, but Blue's hands gentled his resistance, and he rode next to the big man on the cream stallion into a nearby abode village, forming their own parade. The brown accepted the bit and arched his neck from pride and excitement.

The next morning, almost at noon, Blue rode out from the small village to the multitude of good wishes. His head ached, his belly bloated from too much eating and drinking. Yet deep inside, away from the world, he held the notion of a new friend. A *compadre*, a big man on a cream stallion, who now claimed ownership of a fast race horse, the fastest in the small valley nestled close to the dark side of the long mountains.

The valley quickly flattened and was swept into the plains. Blue crossed and recrossed numerous streams, a blessing even in late winter. He luxuriated in the abundance of water, conscious of the deserts left behind him, the taste of dust still in his mouth. He stopped often to drink from the cold streams and wipe the iced water on his face and hands.

But it was too cold, even midday, to take many baths. He tried once, shucking his stinking clothes and determined to wash both them and himself in a wide pool near a stand of cottonwoods. He froze mid-stride; his feet ached, and his belly pulled back to his ribs. There wasn't much choice left; he'd thrown in his clothes and had to retrieve them. His body shook and his toes curled, frozen to the bottom of the stream. Goddamn, it was cold!

The next day, he topped a ridge and saw tailings from a mine, his first landmark for the town of Cimarron. Smith said there was mining, dying out now but part of the town, drawing men eager for quick money. Smith asked him, head cocked, eyes bland, if Blue'd ever been drawn to mining and get-rich-quick, and Blue had surprised neither of them with his answer. It wasn't money that prodded him to ride over the next hill; it wasn't fame and riches. It was only sunlight and cool air, hot desert wind, cactus and tall pines, pine needles piled deep for a new bed, lush graze for the horses, deer watering at a pool, bears circling with dinner in mind.

Going deep into the earth and digging blind wasn't Blue's idea of living. Even as he remembered the strange question, Blue rubbed the still-tender bullet hole and breathed deep, felt the lift and fall of his chest, and tasted his own freedom.

He veered east from the mine tailings, anticipating the clear track to ford the river. The sights of town were on his left now, and he wasn't even tempted to ride in. He was particular about his pleasure; his butt was sore, his belt tugged another notch against his belly, and the taste of whiskey burned in his throat. This town could wait.

The brown gelding nodded his head in agreement, and the jingle of the bit chains and the flash of silver amused Blue. He touched the brown lightly, and they stepped onto the flat road. It was four miles, more or less, Martin Smith said, four miles from the river crossing to the Broken S. The brown drifted into a long trot, and they passed good grass, heavy stands of cottonwoods marking the river's course, an occasional high ridge or deep cut in the land to break the sameness. It was pretty country. If he were a jealous man, Blue thought, a man always wanting more, he could look hard on the likes of Martin Smith, who could claim ownership to miles of this land. Smith had told Blue of Lucien Maxwell, who once set out his marker for over a million acres of the territory. The number was useless to Blue, a boundary no man could set hold of, a measure no man could take and use.

The dirt road forked, the left track lightly dusted with prints of shod horses and slow-stepping cattle. Barbed wire formed square pastures; Blue winced at the barrier and slowed the brown to a walk. He had no old timer's quarrel with the wire, but a good horseman cringed from what those barbs did to his fine stock. Horses couldn't reason out with man's temperament what the barbs meant to them. They feared entrapment; they panicked and ran blindly into the barbed torture, shredding muscle and breaking bones.

So Martin Smith used wire; Blue wondered at what cost to his hot-blooded English stock. Then he made the final turn along the dirt road and saw wood fences crossed beneath old trees. Behind the sturdy fence were heavy-bellied mares, ripe for spring birthing. Blue halted and let the brown quiet. His hands resting on the horn, Blue watched the scene before him for a long moment. The mares moved deliberately in the new grass, six of them, dark chestnuts and solid bays; it was a gift for Blue, to be hired to work such horses. He laughed, and the brown gelding raised his head, his bit chiming in response. Then horse and rider jogged into the avenue leading to a high gate branded with a Broken S.

One man stood near a small corral. Blue nodded to the indistinct figure and received a slow greeting in return. He walked the brown close, reined in, and waited. The man was an Indian, dark-skinned, black hair cut in missionary style, clothes a mix of Indian and white man. The man watched Blue yet did not stare or meet his gaze.

Blue recognized the tactic and knew it was for him to begin. "Name's Blue Mitchell. This Martin Smith's ranch? Been hired by him."

Not much, but enough. The Indian's mouth lifted almost to a smile, and the dark head swung around. The unexpected hazel eyes contained a hidden amusement. "Yes, the big horse tamer, who will ride these animals we cannot. Yes, señor. You are expected. Get down. I will show you where to put your horses. I have been waiting for you. What has taken you so long to ride only a few miles?"

It would be easy to take quick offense to the words, but the light in those hazel eyes and the half smile on the thin mouth taunted Blue, teased him into watching his temper. He shook his head, trimmed his too-ready anger. "I'm here now, can't do much more than that."

The two men watched each other, taking measure, judging out of past experience. Blue shook his head, guessing at the Indian's thoughts. He gently touched the brown gelding's neck before he spoke. "Horse here brought me a good distance, deserves a rest. Packhorse, too. Even if you ain't keen on me, you can't argue with giving these two what's due 'em." He gestured toward the corral, where hay was freshly piled in a wooden manger. "You plannin' on munchin' that hay all by yourself, or you willin' to share with these two broncs?"

He grinned through his words, letting the Indian make the choice. And he guessed there was an edge to the choosing. The Indian's eyes strayed to the strands of blond hair hanging out from Blue's hat, and his hand rested on a wicked sheathed

14

knife. Blue stirred in the saddle, then took a second look at the dark face, and his grin widened. He took the gamble from reading those eyes and dismounted stiffly from the brown, not flinching even when by necessity his back was exposed to the mercy of the Indian's temper and the speed of the long knife still sheathed.

When he touched ground, his sore leg buckled under him, and he stumbled into the brown's belly. Caught half-asleep, the brown cow-kicked and missed Blue's leg, grazing the hard leather chaps. Blue pulled at the saddle horn to steady his wobbly legs and finally turned to face the silent figure watching him.

"The señor, he has hired a pretty boy to work his horses. He is usually smart about how he spends money. You, you who we are told is to ride these fine horses. You cannot even step off your horse without falling down. Those are not mustangs in his fields and stables—those are horses who will eat a pretty boy for breakfast. They will not let a poor man touch them. Nor will the señor pay for bad work. This will be interesting, to see what you will do."

The speech was long and harsh, and the Indian was educated, Blue knew that much about him. As if to ease the tension, the Indian touched the fancy bridle. "So, you have met Señor Martinez. He does not give out this work easily." Blue watched the eyes and the knife still in its sheath and decided a truce had been offered.

He wasn't ready for the pretty girl who appeared to his right, close to the big house. She walked with short delicate steps, her head tilted, her eyes shaded with a slender hand. Blue was suddenly big and clumsy and couldn't hold the reins to the brown or the lead to the placid sorrel. The Indian actually laughed at Blue, then quickly leaned down, picked up the reins, and gave them back, with no more judgment in his face or unsaid words. The Indian, too, was intent on the pretty girl's journey toward them.

When he finally spoke up, the low sound of his voice was enough to spook Blue. "Cowboy, she does not belong to the likes of us. She is the daughter of this ranch. She is a child,

15

and has lost her mother only these few months past. The old man told you, did he not, when he spoke of the horses?"

Blue answered the question. "Yeah, said somethin', but not much. Said nothin' about a child, a daughter . . ."

"We both know our place—it is to speak politely when asked but to offer nothing. You know the rules, as I do." Blue heard the voice continue and felt the strength of the Indian's warning, but he had not seen a pretty child like this one before. Not coming straight at him, eyes shining, hair red-colored and flowing around her face. Innocence walked with the child, sweetness in the pale eyes, youth in the slender form only beginning to show her impending womanhood.

Blue dragged his gaze away from her and muttered his agreement to his motionless companion. As if she could read his mind, the girl stopped abruptly, and Blue almost felt the heat of her shame rush through her. She put both hands to her face and dropped her head, sighed so that Blue and the unnamed Indian could not help but hear her, and retreated back into the confines and safety of the ranch house.

In the next brief minutes, Blue learned that the Indian's name was Peter Charley, that he had worked for Martin Smith for more than five years, and that the small cabin where Blue would live had been built by Peter Charley through one mild winter.

He learned nothing more about the girl, nothing more about Peter Charley or the rest of the ranch hands or working cowboys. The horses were released into their new confinement, the cabin was opened, and Blue's meager belongings were piled inside. Word was brought down by an ancient, shriveled man that Blue was wanted at the main house whenever it was convenient for him.

Through the commotion and the readjustment, the image of the young girl walking toward him interfered and blocked out much of what was said to him, until Peter Charley grabbed his forearm, shook him, and stepped back quickly to allow the anticipated blow to pass by his face harmlessly. Off balance, angry, and tired, Blue had to listen to the Indian one more time.

"She is a child playing a woman's game, Señor Blue. She can look like what you wish her to be. Do not be fooled; do not listen. Remember the laws and stick to them, and forget what you think of the girl. She is a picture, a story. She is not real."

The impact of Peter Charley's knowing voice caught Blue unprepared. He had expected a warning, a short fight, anything but to be told the lovely child was dangerous. He half turned from the Indian and ran the words over in his mind. They were a clear warning, and not a good one. He wanted only to do his work and get paid. Not to play nursemaid to a pretty child.

He walked toward the ranch house, ready to quit right then if anyone came to give him more orders.

TWO

THE FINE-BONED CHESTNUT filly jumped across the corral, head high, ears flat to her head. For a brief moment it looked as if she would take one more stride, jump the fence, and break her neck. Martin Smith wanted to yell at the motionless man inside the corral, order him to do anything to keep the filly from getting damaged. Instead, Smith forced himself only to watch and keep his mouth closed. He had paid this man good wages to work the horses; now he had to trust in his own judgment and be quiet.

The filly slid to a stop, whirled, and stood motionless. Her body quivered in fright, and lather showed along her neck and chest. Nothing moved in the corral; the filly waited and the man on the porch waited with her.

Then the source of the filly's distress began to walk, taking small steps, moving slowly, hestitantly. The filly trembled violently but held her ground. Smith could see one arm outstretched, could almost hear the deep voice talk its nonsense words. Smith half smiled, a bitter movement of his lips; he could see now why the men in the long bunkhouse spoke with contempt for this strange man who claimed mastery over unwilling horses.

The horse tamer had stopped; the filly's ears were pricked forward, her eyes bright enough for Martin Smith to watch. Smith fancied he could hear the sounds issued from the young man's mouth. Sounds with no meaning, meant to work a

18

magic not yet in evidence. The filly was the first horse this Blue Mitchell had worked for Martin Smith; he had stood with her in the same corral yesterday, talking only, not approaching the filly, not dragging out a rope or even a halter and lead line. The filly had come close once, that first day, and had kicked at the horse tamer, then spun around and tried to bite him. Mitchell had only moved quickly out of range but had not taken the fight back to the filly.

Martin Smith was beginning to agree with the majority of his men, that this Blue Mitchell was a bust, that the money had been spent foolishly and that Mitchell would be off the ranch before nightfall. Only Peter Charley said to wait, watch, learn from Mitchell; only Peter Charley saw what no one else could understand.

The filly's head went higher; Smith heard her fearful snort and damned the cattleman who'd recommended Mitchell, then damned himself for listening. And firing him so soon would reflect on his judgment, or lack thereof. Smith rubbed his bald head and snorted with the filly, disgusted at the entire situation.

He was immediately aware of the footsteps behind him and deliberately watched the scene being played out in the corral. Without turning to see, he spoke to his daughter, his voice low and sympathetic. "Luisa says we are low on certain staples, so I believe a trip into town is necessary. Would you care to accompany me, my dear?" Smith was too conscious of trying to divert his Flora; she was quick to speak her mind, even in indelicate matters, and he did not wish to hear what would be said next. But mention of the excursion did little to put Flora off track.

"Papa, he is doing nothing but chasing that poor filly around and around. Look, he's standing there with no bridle or rope, nothing. As if she will simply walk up to him and bow down in amazement."

There were times when Flora's abrupt manner could be disconcerting. She was sweet, generally, and still innocent of the world. Yet she could set off words that flayed the heart and soul of a man. Smith at that moment was glad he was not a self-proclaimed horse tamer surrounded by a frightened chestnut filly and a strong-willed girl.

Yet he came to Mitchell's defense, out of his own pride at having hired the man and a respect for Peter Charley's few words. "Give him time, my dear. I was told he is most unorthodox, so we will wait a bit longer. Perhaps we will learn something after all."

In companionable silence, father and daughter studied the slow activity in the corral. The father remained in his chair, and the daughter stood directly behind him, her fine hands resting on the chair back. Seen in such patient posing, their likeness was in evidence. Fine regular features, a strong chin, smooth high cheeks. The hair of the girl was a soft red-brown, the father was graying and balding, but the tilt of their heads and the intensity of their stares were strong reminders of their close kinship.

The filly whinnied, a shrill, plaintive sound that stirred both father and child to shake their heads in unison.

Blue hummed quietly, shoulders slumped, hand raised, legs widespread and solid. It was almost that time, the filly lowered her head, snorted again in warning, then, seeing no threat, pushed her muzzle out in youthful curiosity. The object before her, the figure of a man, showed no interest or concern in her behavior. She took one step, then another, then stretched her neck until her long chin whiskers swept over the outstretched hand.

The hum became louder, but the filly was no longer afraid. The noise was a comfort, a balm to her rattled temper. She took one step, and the edge of her muzzle rested on the flesh of the man, then pushed into the cup of the palm and fingers of his hand. The smell intrigued her; the fingers wiggled against her whiskered lips, and she withdrew, snorting lightly. Then she reached out and licked the palm. The salty taste pleased her. She pushed hard with her muzzle, opened her lips, and let her teeth touch skin.

The sound grew sharp, a warning the filly accepted. She bit down on the hand and jumped back, stood away from her victim and watched carefully. The man did not move, did not threaten her. She came back, reached out, and the palm cupped her mouth. Then the second hand stretched to rub the flesh of the filly's neck. The motion was soothing, rubbing sweaty skin, and the filly leaned into the motion, slowly relaxing.

The touch was curiously pleasant to the filly; her eyes closed, her head dropped, and she enjoyed the hand as it moved across her neck, rubbed her chest, and then her prominent withers. Pressure weighed the crest of her neck. She raised her head against it, but the voice droned on and she relaxed again. Two hands stroked the flat of her jowl, then firmed on her tender nose. She did not like that touch, but the voice calmed her, told her she was still safe. A lighter touch encircled her nose, then behind her ears, and the filly stiffened and opened her eyes, but the halter was quickly buckled, and the man holding the rope made no more sudden moves. The filly shook her head, and the leather tickled but did not hurt.

Until she pulled back and the man held to the soft lead rope and talked to her. Pressure pinched her head, and her nose felt raw. The filly half reared and yanked back, but the man held firm and continued talking without making threat or promise.

Quickly bored, the filly stood her ground; white-eyed and ears furiously flipping back and forth, she watched the man before her. There was no change in him, no fear in his smell, no demand other than that she accept the weight around her head.

The man came closer to her; the filly flinched, and the pressure returned to her tender head. She waited, wary now but willing to find out. That hand touched her, began to stroke her along her neck and rub her chest, even sweep along her ribs and hindquarters. The filly allowed the intimacy, her head lowered, and she began once again to enjoy the process of being tamed.

"Papa, look, she's following him like a dog. She's even letting him lean on her. Pick up a foot, she's bowing like a

21

circus pony. What did he do?'' Flora's voice rose to a shrill note, and Martin Smith held up a finger to his mouth. ''Shhhh, Flora.'' As if the horse and its new master could hear them. ''Shhh.''

It was indeed unorthodox, as the man had said. And Smith bet he could see the grin spread across Peter Charley's face. Smith himself felt as if he could climb on the filly right now and ride her around the confines of the small pen in complete safety and obedience. It would not happen that easily, Smith knew; the filly would not be ridden without some fireworks. But her behavior at this moment amazed him.

Blue turned from the filly and walked to the fence; the filly followed as he knew she would. He climbed three rails, then laid his weight on the filly's back. She set her ears back but waited, listened while Blue told her what he was going to do. Her tension dissolved quickly; Blue put more of his weight on her. When she finally became nervous and distressed, Blue slid off, gently pushing her away from him. The filly raised a hind foot in warning, and Blue laughed, patting her dry neck. The filly stuck out her nose and was rewarded with a pat, a pull of her long whiskers.

Martin Smith watched in amazed admiration; he was not too far wrong in believing that the filly could now be ridden. He waited in anticipation, but Mitchell disappeared from the corral, and the filly quickly dozed in the late sun. Smith talked to his daughter without looking back to see if she was listening. ''My dear, I do believe this man will earn his wages after all. I have never seen the like, never.''

But his Flora was not behind him to hear his words. She had retreated into the concealment of her private rooms, a curious smile frozen on her pinched face. She wondered if the man's touch on the chestnut filly could be transferred to the body of a willing woman.

The following day Martin Smith rode to Cimarron for business concerns. The banker had asked for his advice on several matters. It was not Smith's choice to be involved with banking, but he felt an obligation to the town he could not put aside merely for his own fleeting pleasure.

When he returned early evening, having spent an hour or two with friends at the St. James Hotel, he found Flora walking through the house in darkness. He was momentarily disturbed, for her eyes shone and her face burned in a fever that frightened him. She had been a sickly child, trying the patience of his dear wife, Elizabeth, until a series of local ladies were hired to ease the burden. Now, that excitement had come back into Flora's manner, and Martin Smith was dismayed.

"He rode that filly today, Papa. He rode her as if she had been saddled and ridden all her life. He's good, Papa, he's very clever." Then her voice trailed away, and her eyes dimmed. The whiskey consumed by her father allowed him to dismiss her agitation. She was not ill, that was all he could sum up from their unlikely conservation—that she was not ill and that Blue Mitchell had ridden the chestnut filly.

His head ached the next morning, and he was still preoccupied with the business matters that had taken him to Cimarron. More of the mines were in financial trouble, especially Albert Buckminster's Cutheart. The problems were not of a serious nature, but combined with the pounding in his head and the bright skies, Smith did not get out to the veranda to watch his horse tamer until past midday. Flora was there, intent on watching the strange cowboy still at his game with the filly. She did not look up at her father's approach, nor did she acknowledge him until he forcefully took her two hands in his and asked how she was on this fine day. She merely shook her head and vaguely waved, then settled back to watch Blue Mitchell.

He rode the filly in a heavy hackamore, with his hands widespread to direct her uncertain movements. The saddle was stripped down, carrying a single cinch and no rope, no slicker tied behind the cantle or rifle stuck in its boot. The filly's uneasiness was plain to see; she could not trot in a straight line, nor could she balance around a corner. But her eyes were calm, her neck relaxed as she carried her new burden.

"He is good, Papa. And so odd-looking, almost handsome." The words were normal, but Martin Smith misread the tone of his dear child and only agreed with her assessment. Blue Mitchell was good with the horses; Smith had no more doubts.

It was two more months before the thoroughbreds were ready to ride, and the team of part-Morgans came in from their own reschooling. Now Martin Smith felt the team was safe for his Flora to drive when she chose. Smith sold three of the thoroughbreds to a rancher in Colorado and one as a racehorse to a man from Chicago. His reputation as a breeder of good stock was rapidly spreading, and Martin Smith duly accepted the acclaim. There were three saddle horses and a racer, all with his name on their papers. He thought to mention Blue Mitchell's talent in training these horses, but the conversations did not always turn in such a manner as to introduce the subject. Still, Martin Smith thought he would pay the man a good bonus.

It occurred to Smith that he perhaps should take a closer look at Mitchell when he realized how much time his daughter was spending watching the man work with the horses. He queried Peter Charley about the man's daily habits, and for a while kept an eye on Flora, but he could see no contact between the two young people. Mitchell made no friends among the cowhands on Smith's payroll, other than to talk for short periods with Peter Charley. Mitchell rode the horses out along the river or schooled them in circles in the larger round pen. He even shook out a rope and got the horses used to its presence.

But Mitchell was not seen around the girl, nor in contact with anyone on the ranch. He was not particularly unfriendly, only remote from the daily routine. He seemed to find his work with the horses enough and kept to himself otherwise, much to Smith's eventual relief. He would have to write that cattleman near Santa Fe and thank him for the casual reference.

He had recognized the stallion was trouble when the big youngster turned two years old. There was racing in the colt's bloodlines and fire in his heart. Martin Smith often went down to the private pen in the evenings, when his Elizabeth was sleeping in some comfort and no longer needed his attention. He stood outside the high fence and watched the beauty of the colt. The coat shone like new flame, the dark eyes glowed a banked fire, and the hard legs skidded in clouds of dirt as the impatient animal circled the confining pen.

As a gift that spring, a neighbor had offered a small brown-and-white puppy to occupy Flora through her mother's illness. Flora called the animal Tops, and every evening he walked with Martin to the corrals. Smith paid scant attention to the small dog; his mind was set on his wife's fading, his daughter's growing, the terrible aloneness he was not used to feeling. He would laugh at the pup's antics. Tops made no demands and asked only to be good company.

One evening Tops grew bold enough to enter the colt's prison. The pup stayed near the fence and did not bark or tease the young stallion, and Smith paid the dog little mind. Instead he leaned on the skinned poles and rested his face on his arm, inhaling the scent of fresh pine, hearing the muffled sound of the stallion's hooves. It was his rare time of peace.

He heard the squeal and looked up to see the colt strike out. The pup was mangled, its head shapeless, its small body quickly drained of blood. Smith alone buried the pup and found himself crying softly over the new grave. He ached intensely, his hands trembled, and his brain sorted through emotions he would not ordinarily allow in himself or others.

He could not tell the entire truth; he fabricated that Tops had annoyed the colt until the animal struck back in ancient protective instinct. Flora did cry, and her father allowed her the display for a brief while, then handed her a white kerchief

25

and told her to wipe her eyes, go check on her mother. It had only been a dog, after all.

He recognized then the evil of the chestnut stallion, but as he reread the colt's ancestry, he made silent excuses to himself for the action and promised himself that he would find an uncommon man to train the colt, one who could wipe out all traces of that primitive streak and bend the chestnut colt to human standards.

He forgot his own promise to himself in the ensuing months. He forgot almost everything except the need to be with his dying Elizabeth and to calm his restless, hysterical daughter.

Then, the winter the chestnut turned four, Smith was given the name of a man who could work miracles. Blue Mitchell was hired, and Martin Smith sat back to watch.

THREE

THE GIRL DREW him in, wrapped herself around his thoughts until he could not sleep at night. She did nothing to deserve this infatuation; she was pure and sweet. But he could not keep his mind from images of her. She laughed gently, smiled often, and asked continual questions. There was little pride or devious behavior in her. She sat with her father and watched Blue work the horses, and he was completely, foolishly in love.

He had to admit she was skilled with the young stock, the weaned foals and yearlings, but she had been badly taught to ride, and he would wish to retrain her. But the thought of coming too close to her unnerved him, and he instinctively kept his distance. The line was drawn, detailed, well known and accepted. He would look, and dream, but he would never touch.

Even the father had some idea of what was in Blue's mind—he had to, for the words he spoke were not the usual ones. The talk had begun with details about the chestnut colt, apologies almost for the colt being four and untrained. It had come during his wife's illness, Smith said, and Blue shied from the pain clear in the man's eyes. That was no excuse, Smith acknowledged, but it was the plain truth. The colt had escaped his future until the spring of his fourth year, and it would be more difficult for Blue now, harder on the colt, too, to begin schooling meant to be already finished.

The talk turned queer then and backed Blue some distance from Martin Smith. As if there were things unsaid that troubled Smith but could not be spoken. The words were blunt, but it was the hidden meaning that spooked Blue. Everything, Martin Smith said, everything at some point in its existence had to accept the fact that others in the human community made the decisions, that mankind was truly the master and no true free spirit existed within the bounds of the human world.

Blue imagined Smith was talking straight at him then, and not just about the big chestnut colt. He half turned to walk away, allowing anger and pride to rise quickly inside him. His mouth flooded with a sour taste; no one owned him, no one tamed him unless he allowed it.

Then he thought of the girl and came close to an understanding; she caught him with her smile and fluttering hands. He had stood for the rope around his neck and was now willing to be saddled and ridden. Over a mere girl and the promise of gold coin and printed paper.

The thinking on those words drove Blue to restless wandering. He stepped off from Smith's talk, conscious of the clean air smudged by wood smoke and sweat, human scent and rotting garbage. Blue shuddered, scared by a deep course of thought he had not known before. He needed action, fight, turmoil, and risky chances to blot out what had settled deep inside him.

His escape was close to perfect until Martin Smith put a hand on his forearm and whispered words Blue felt closed an open door. "You won't touch my child, will you? You know the rules; you know how fragile she is. She's all I have now, with her mother gone, her brothers. . . . Mitchell, you understand?"

The words uttered in hushed confidence rattled Blue; he itched suddenly like a hard-ridden bronc. He needed miles between him and these people, who talked friendly and laid claims he'd never even seen. His impulse was to saddle and ride.

Instead he walked to the corral, where four men and two

stout workhorses had pulled in the chestnut stallion. It had taken two hours to rope and drag the stubborn horse. Now the stallion stalked the edge of his prison, stopping to rest the tip of his nose on the top rail. The fence was six feet of lashed poles and stout posts; Blue looked between railings and saw the colt, the dark patches of sweat on the neck and chest, between the hind legs. The long tail lashed back and forth, setting a rebellious pattern. The head bobbed in time with the arrogant gait as the colt continued his pace.

Then, as if something rank in the air came to him, the colt stopped, whirled, reared high, and slammed his forelegs on the hard-packed earth. The colt focused on Blue, the dark eyes white-rimmed, the fine nostrils expanding to draw in Blue's scent. The colt snorted, reared again, pumped the hot air through his lungs, and struck out with a forefoot. Blue had been challenged.

Blue jerked back; Flora Smith stood next to him. He could almost hear her heart pound as she watched the chestnut stallion. Her hazel eyes glowed with excitement, her face was flushed, and her hands trembled where they rested on the rail. She frightened Blue, more than the known power and fury of the trapped colt. When she spoke, her voice was low, thick, older than her years. "He is beautiful, isn't he. Magnificent. He would like to kill you, Blue. Just you. He's beautiful."

She was so young, he thought, so young she did not know what she was saying. The horse had no personal grudge, not like a wronged human. The horse challenged the world around him, not Blue Mitchell alone. The chestnut reared again, and Blue watched through the railings; it came suddenly to him that in the next few days this horse could kill him. It was a new feeling, an awe he had never known. It panicked him, and he tried to cover his raw reaction.

"He sure is a pretty one, ain't he, miss." God, he thought, I sound like a dumb school kid. A right fool. But he couldn't stop. "He won't be much trouble, all that fussin's for show. I worked with stud horses, already run mares, got them used to saddle and bit. That little colt, he won't be much."

Pure bravado and full-drawn wrong. That colt was one in a million for Blue, and he knew it. But the words stuck in his throat and came out as stupid and dumbstruck as he felt.

The little girl saw right through him and added to his own humiliation. "Why, Blue Mitchell, you are bragging. You know as well as I do that you are afraid. I bet you won't be able to ride that chestnut. I bet you he will throw you first try. Why, Mr. Mitchell, anyone can see that colt is too strong, far too intelligent to put up with the likes of you."

He was hard struck. His belly went hollow, and his hands ached. He had thought she was young, sweet, yet here, now, she was pushing at him, challenging him, daring him to reckless acts. He'd been fooled, blinded by looks and imagings. Caught in his own fantasy. Skinned out and quartered and cooked slow over a fire. He looked sideways at the pretty girl, saw the flush still on her cheeks, the thread of excitement shining in her eyes. He tried to explain, knowing full well he could only make a bigger fool of himself. "Miss, I apologize. You're right. That colt, why, he takes my breath. He's pure wild, pure instinct. Ain't no man going to tame that one. Ride him, maybe. But not tame."

She had come close to him as he spoke, and now he could feel the heat of her. The tipped point of her bosom rubbed his arm, and he inhaled hot air, gulped and swallowed. She paid no attention to his unrest but spoke only of what she wanted. "Blue, please. Hold me. I've never felt this way, not with all the young men courting me with Papa's blessing. Blue, hold me."

He wanted to tell her it was the raw power of the stallion, the threat of dying, the taste of a coming storm that teased her, but she did not give him the room. "Blue, please hold me." The words were gasped, and Blue tasted them blown into his mouth as she talked to and kissed him. Asking as she took what she wanted, pleasing while she pressed against him, arousing him until he could no longer breathe freely or let her go.

It was a long kiss, long enough that the chestnut colt settled down and finally came close enough to watch. The girl was quick to press against Blue and then move before he could hold her. She was eager to take in his mouth, biting his lip and then sliding away, ducking her face from him in feigned shyness. He brought up one hand, held her chin, and turned her face. Her eyes glowed, and her skin burned his fingers. She leaned forward, denied the strength of his hand, and kissed him again, sighed deeply, and spooked the curious, quieted chestnut colt.

Then she was done playing that game and went to the next; she pirouetted away, spun a circle, and smiled at Blue, tilting her head so her eyes were shaded by her lashes and her hair lay fetchingly across her brow. She had become the tender young thing again, the innocent and inexperienced. The little girl so beloved by her unseeing father.

"Blue, teach me to ride. Really ride, not trot around on that stupid sidesaddle wearing a heavy skirt and those gloves, that silly veil. I've watched you when you take one of the horses out along the river. I've seen the horse run full speed. It looks wonderful, it must feel . . . like this, tonight. Blue, teach me, please."

The chestnut colt had centuries of temper in him. Well bred, well born and fed, sheltered in cold weather and hot, pastured on lush grass, he had suffered no hunger, felt no discomfort in his four years. He had grown proud, convinced of his immortality.

Now he was stronger, wilder, ready to mount the mares that would be his for the taking, ready to control and cover the mares taken from another stallion. He only had to lift his head and the wind brought him their scent, the deep musk that said they were ready for him. His eyes glazed, his body trembled, and blood pulsed through him until he was fully ready. His long stride brought him to the offending fence, all that stood between him and the mares. He reared high and screamed in anger and frustration. His life was outside this captive fence, his life called from the green grass and the rushing river, the raised tails and willing stance of the blooded mares.

The hated figure came too close to the fence; the man smell was harsh and bitter. The chestnut stallion reared and struck out. The tormenter leaned on the prison bars and did nothing more. The colt rammed his body against the fence repeatedly, once catching a stronger sense of the man waiting for him. The man laughed and stepped back when the colt again issued his challenge. Again and again the chestnut colt bullied the fence, and still the man only watched and talked to the enraged horse.

Finally exhausted, the stallion retreated to the center of the corral and glared through dust-reddened eyes at the man still leaning on the fence. Human and horse watched each other, taking measure, neither stepping back, neither giving in. They recognized their opponent in the battle yet to come.

Then there were two days of isolation, where the chestnut had only water and scant food and no sounds of the human's voice, no sight of the human's form. Only the scent of the tantalizing mares was left to remind him of what was beyond the corral.

Martin Smith was called to Denver on business. Banker's troubles, he said, a fool's errand yet one he could not deny. Blue drove him into Cimarron, where he was to catch a stage-coach. On the drive, Smith strayed from any important talk and kept to the bland topic of needing a railroad into the town, or how well the team of part-Morgans was doing, the necessity of having some kind of permanent irrigation system to not be so dependent on the vagaries of the weather. Blue half listened, understanding only some of the big words. Other thoughts crowded his mind.

Until Smith's voice cracked and Blue paid attention. Age caught up with everyone, the man said. And there were no exceptions. The words made Blue shake like no rank bronc or raised fist had ever done. He had only to look at his companion, seated on the high buckboard seat, he had only to count the lines of the man's face and see the deep tiredness in the eyes to fully know the truth of the spoken thought.

He left Smith at the St. James Hotel, picked up a waiting

package of supplies from the general store, and returned to the now-familiar ground of the Broken S and his new adversaries, the chestnut colt and the pretty, fragile girl.

It was decided to wait until Martin Smith returned from Denver before Blue would tackle the chestnut. Smith expressed his desire to be a spectator at the initial encounters, and Blue could not refuse: the man paid out his wage.

He was left with days waiting to be filled, time endlessly expansive in front of him, filled now only with nightmares of the chestnut stallion and fantasies of the flighty girl.

Peter Charley saw the same story and came five steps from Blue, cleared his throat, and looked out toward the river, the distant mountains, anywhere except at Blue's face. It was a courtesy, yet it was obvious Peter Charley had something of importance to say.

The Indian spoke direct, clear, with no mistake; it was not the habit of his ancestors or his own way, but the words forced him to speak so. "Blue, the stallion is a deliberate killer. He is not wild; he is a throwback, a return to other times." There was silence then, to allow Blue full understanding. Peter Charley walked to a nearby fence, leaned on its support, and fashioned a smooth cigarette from papers and cut tobacco. Blue followed, the information rolling over in his mind. But the Indian gave him no time for argument.

"And the girl, she is not what you think. And not what her father wishes her to be. I have seen, I have watched and known. She, too, is from the past, when it was right to take without giving, for survival, for life."

Blue swung his head around, and Peter Charley answered, "I am mission-educated, Blue Mitchell. But I am also Jicarilla Apache. Both worlds are inside me, as they are in you. I am not telling you what you do not already know. Be careful."

The Indian extended the cigarette. Blue pulled deeply, held in the smoke, and then allowed it to escape slowly. Peter Charley nodded and repeated Blue's gestures. The cigarette was shared until Blue's fingertips were singed. The stallion screamed from his cage, and both men felt the sound knife through them. As they separated, Peter Charley spoke his last words. "Be careful—of the stallion and the girl, Blue Mitchell."

One hour later, Flora Smith appeared by the horse pen; her fine auburn hair was braided up and tied, and her feet were in high boots. Blue could not look at her; she wore a pair of dark wool pants and a white shirt, a soft leather jacket, clothes meant for a boy, clothes she would not wear with her father's approval. But Martin Smith was in Denver.

"Please, Blue, let me ride with you. I know the horse you have saddled is silly in company and you want to cure him of that. I've listened, I've seen you. Let me ride with you. Teach me."

He eased his conscience by telling a tale that the eager gelding could do with company. He chose a solid bay for Miss Flora to ride; the horse could teach manners to the flighty gray. It was a good excuse, but Blue's stomach still ached.

The girl was silent beside him as they rode out, and Blue concentrated on the young gray. Bears hid behind trees, goblins hung from branches, and skeletons rattled from wind-blown bushes. Blue was hard-pressed to keep the horse under control. He could not help but laugh at the gelding's antics, and finally Miss Flora's light voice joined in the amusement.

The gray tired suddenly and found it was easy to walk sedately beside the calm bay. It was possible now for Blue to approach the subject of horsemanship. "Miss?" He tried to speak gently, not wishing to set the gray off again. "Miss, if you let out your reins some, that bay'll be happy, carry you better. He ain't going nowhere, you let him do his job." Just like a dumb farm kid, still, as if he did not know a secret about Miss Flora Smith.

The girl didn't bother to look at him, but her hand opened and the reins slid, and when the bay dropped his head and sighed deeply, both the girl and Blue had to laugh. "Poor thing," she said, "I've been terrible to him." Blue relaxed. She was a pretty thing, and she had feelings for the horse she

34

rode. Maybe what had happened a few nights back was more mixed up than he thought. Maybe Peter Charley was wrong.

Her face was saddened, and Blue tried to help. "No, miss, you ain't hurt him none. You only been making work out of what's pleasure." She came around in the saddle then, and Blue knew he had been wrong.

"Mr. Mitchell, I cannot imagine where you would get the idea that a rancher and his family ride for pleasure. Hard work made the Broken S, and my father and I continue to work hard. Please don't ever make that mistake again."

Blue drew back from the force of the words, and the gray under him responded by stopping dead. The girl on the bay kept on going, head high, shoulders back. Blue sat the restive gray and enjoyed the picture, but he was puzzled by her words. He had worked the Broken S for over two months now and had not once seen the girl out of her flimsy dresses, working in the garden or driving a team, hanging wet clothes, or even cooking raised bread. He did not understand the fury of her words at all.

The gray quickly caught up with the other horse, and Blue tried to make his apologies. "Miss, all I got to say, you make being ridden easier on a bronc, he'll have more to give back. More work in him if that's all you want."

They rode for an hour more, working on signals to turn the horses, change gaits, slide into quick stops. The girl was attentive, a quick pupil, and Blue found he enjoyed the exercise.

Finally the girl stopped her bay and stared openly at Blue. "Why is it so important to you that the horse do all these things? Why does it matter that he go this way or that—what good is it? I've watched you and listened to you, and you seem to think this is all magic, like being part of the horse you ride. I only want to gallop along the river, the way I've seen you do. Not twist and turn and jump this way and that. I'm tired."

Blue spoke flat out, without thinking first. "Miss, when you got a man with a cocked pistol coming at you, full-fired and primed, you damn well want your horse to cut out fast,

35

and where you point him. Can mean your life, if that horse don't listen. Can mean a few more years, you got a good one knows his training.''

To his ears the words were crude, harsh, but they carried all that he meant to say. He'd been in that kind of trouble, where his old age was most likely to be cut short. A good horse kept a man alive; a good rifle added a few years more.

Blue looked at the openmouthed girl, and it occurred to him at that moment. A girl like this one, she could right quick shorten the odds on a man living to full term.

Some of his thinking must have showed, for Miss Flora Smith arched her back and kicked at the bay, swinging the horse in a small circle. ''Blue Mitchell, you are mad. I like it. Let's race, let's run along the river.'' And she was gone, three strides out before Blue got his legs and hands working and the gray thoroughbred settled down to run.

Flora had ridden most of her life; even her delicate mother had seen the benefits of the fresh air and exercise for her darling child. But Flora had never sat a horse this way, never felt the powerful body so close between her legs. Her hands touched the arched neck, and she could smell the strands of black mane that whipped her face. Blue Mitchell had given her this, as much as he had showed her how to sit in the saddle and control the horse, ask for a slow walk, demand more speed.

Speed was a drug. She never wanted to slow down, stop the running. The sound inside her was eerie; the wind at her ears, the rush of air over her lips, the tears in her wide eyes. The distant, steady pound of the horses' hooves spoke to her; pure freedom, power, and speed.

The horses came back to a walk at Mitchell's command. Flora wanted to deny him, but she saw the foam on the gray gelding and felt the rapid heaving of her own horse and knew the animals were tired. They were merely earthbound; she had flown high at their expense.

Flora determinedly slowed her breathing, allowing herself to wake up to her surroundings. Her pulse still pounded in her ear, and her body was wet, soaked from exhilaration. The wildness almost released was recaptured, but it waited inside for her now, waited for the next time.

Mitchell guided them to the river bank, intending to let the horses drink. The sound of their greedy sucking made Flora quite thirsty. She dismounted, dropped the reins with no more thought, knelt on the river's edge, and plunged her hands into the cold water. She drank from her cupped hands and smiled at Blue Mitchell as the water ran down her arms, fell from her open mouth, and spotted the front of her white shirt. Mitchell stared at her only for a moment, and once again she looked into those odd, unreadable eyes and felt the wildness come up inside her. The man was as untrained as his horses, barely tamed, just broken to the bit and spur of a woman's fancy. Blue Mitchell was no better than the horses he rode, no more saddle-wise than the chestnut stallion that waited for him in the high-walled corral. Flora smiled, then buried her face in the river water.

FOUR

MARTIN SMITH WAS there. He'd been back two days from Denver, where all words spoken had saddened him. He intended to watch his horse tamer work the chestnut stallion and planned to use the spectacle as recuperation from the long miles traveled and the insight into men's minds that disturbed him.

He was there, seated on the long veranda in his favorite chair, a glass at hand, a cigar gone cold in his mouth, when the chestnut stallion committed his murderous deed.

Mitchell roped out the horse, using a slow loop that barely spooked the colt. It was as if the time in isolation had mellowed the chestnut's fury, softened his inherent anger. Mitchell didn't yank the colt down as the loop settled on its proud neck, nor did the man bait the stallion into fighting. He did nothing more than stand and face the fretting horse, with the rope in his loose hands, a short smile on his wind-burned, homely face. Smith could read the expression now; he was more familiar with the man's mind. Mitchell was quiet, determined, and essentially unafraid. So Martin Smith thought as he sipped his choice brandy.

The colt reacted slowly, finally rearing, coming down, rearing again and then going into a spin and running to the end of the rope. Mitchell moved with the horse, never allowing the rope to tighten. The chestnut fought the prison, slamming into the high fence, kicking with both hind legs, rearing again and striking the top rail with one front hoof. During the one-sided battle, Blue Mitchell simply held to the rope and followed the stallion's wild lead. Smith's mind wandered to the Denver meetings, to the harsh words about mine failures and a comment directed at him about some of the poorer elements moving into the town of Cimarron.

Then Mitchell came awake in the corral as the chestnut colt reared high. The man was behind the horse, yanking on the rope, bringing the colt toppling from his high perch. The rope was flipped over the still-racing legs, and the stallion lay imprisoned on the ground.

Martin Smith was taken completely by surprise; Mitchell had never been this forceful with the thoroughbreds. He thought to speak up, ask questions, but then he thought of the bloody corpse of the small dog and kept silent. Mitchell could not know about the pup, but it was as if he sensed that raging power within the stallion. A number of the ranch hands showed their curiosity by edging close to the corral in hushed groups.

But Mitchell did nothing more than leave the corral, the horse tied helplessly on the ground. He went to one of the small groups and must have asked for the makings, for soon he lit up a smoke. Then he went to the pump, drew up water, and ducked his head under the flow. The chestnut colt screamed, and Mitchell showed no discernible interest at the terrible sound.

Soon enough it was evident that nothing more was to happen. The men as quietly went back to their work, and even Smith ducked inside the house, suddenly quite hungry. There was no one to watch except one blank-faced mission Indian when, three hours later, Blue let the stallion out of the confining ropes. The colt staggered on numbed legs, found his balance and reared, struck out at his tormentor, no longer screaming a challenge but snorting deep in his throat.

Peter Charley came to stand near Blue while the horse tamer coiled the long rope and watched the riled-up colt. "He won't forgive you. Ever. He will hate with all that is in him. But you know that. There is not much else you can do to him now.'' There was rough pride in the Indian's statement, as if he now stood connected to Blue.

There was no answer asked for, no comment required. Blue stood and watched the chestnut stallion while Peter Charley rolled a cigarette.

The next day, as Blue entered the corral and fashioned his loop, the chestnut stood and watched, making no effort to fight or run. He accepted the loop around his neck and even took one step when Blue tugged on the line. Blue watched the colt's eyes carefully, judging, weighing what he could see. There was no fear in those eyes, only boredom.

The colt quickly learned to lead around the corral, following the man, stopping on command from the crude halter twisted around his head. Martin Smith and his daughter watched from the veranda and talked of inconsequential matters.

The third day, the morning turned cool and the wind blew softly. A perfect day. Smith brought his late breakfast out on the veranda, and Flora sat beside him, laughing at silly stories her father told about his Denver trip. Occasionally they glanced over at the corral but did not expect much of interest to happen.

Blue roped the chestnut easily and flipped the loose coil that became a halter around the proud head. The colt shied slightly, then stuck out his nose in a gesture of curiosity. Blue tugged on the line, and the colt evidently remembered yesterday's lessons, for he walked forward in response to the command. When there was less than five feet separating horse and man, the chestnut stopped of his own accord, lowered his head, and snorted. The small ears swiveled, and the nostrils distended to draw in the man's scent.

Blue waited, hesitant, concerned about the signs the colt was giving him; warning signs of banked anger, rising fury. The ears suddenly flattened against the damp neck; Blue crooned to the nervous colt and allowed the rope to hang loosely from the extended head.

40

When it seemed right, when the small ears had come forward again and the eyes were calmed, Blue brought his hand out, palm up, offering it to the colt's inspection. The eyes widened but did not show white, the ears remained forward and relaxed, and the fine muzzle rested cautiously on Blue's fingertips.

Flora Smith saw the initial contact and smiled; Blue Mitchell might be half-wild himself, but he could tame the strongest of raging beasts. She touched her father's shoulder so he might look up and see the amazing spectacle.

Then, suddenly, the colt reared and struck out at the man insolent enough to touch him. The hoof cut deep into the side of Blue Mitchell's head close to the temple. The dark, shapeless hat flew off, and the blond hair was quickly stained red. The man collapsed, falling sideways, his head hitting the packed corral floor.

The stallion reared, higher, full of his strength, triumphant, majestic. The noble head rose above the fence, mouth gaping, ears flat, plumed tail in full glory. Then the colt came down, hard, turned back, stopped and snorted, and lowered his head to briefly smell the vanquished foe. The breath of warmed air lifted strands of loosened blond hair, which fell back and covered the gray, pale skull.

The young stallion drew himself up and swelled as he issued a challenge to those who would tame him. The warning sound came too late, after the body of the colt shuddered, deflated, sprawled on the corral floor too close to the unconscious man. At the shot's final echo, each man who had stood and watched the killing swiveled toward the long veranda. They stared at the source of the terrible, lonely sound.

Martin Smith slowly lowered his rifle. The smell of the bullet and the small remaining puff of smoke lingered as the only evidence of his act.

PART
TWO

FIVE

HER PATIENT WAS restless again, and she needed to finish her chores and return to him. She could comfort him, calm him where no one else could. He was so erratic, it was hard to judge when it was right to leave him. Sometimes he lay for hours, unmoving, barely breathing, until she believed his eventual dying just as the doctor had told her. Then he would roll his head or raise his arms weakly as if seeking her, and she would stroke his burning face, say out loud all the words she wished were hers to speak to a man. He must have heard her voice, for he listened and ceased fighting, and then he would return to a restless sleep.

She had once had a man. All too briefly, but long enough to discover the fulfillment of both emotional and physical love. And then God took her man from her, chilled by the winter winds and a river dunking. She tended him religiously, prayed for him, bathed him, sweated out his fever with blankets and warm fire, but in the end he coughed up blood and died.

Her husband had been a kind man; small, balding, with an endearing rounded belly and thick hands, a mouth made for laughter, a mind willing to set to hard work. A small, strange, outspoken man who had sent away for a bride and had completely accepted his bargain.

Thomas Miller had met her at the stage, doffed his hat, and greeted her with flowers. He had not noticed her height, towering over him by at least six inches; he had not worried about her long face or her watery eyes, her thinning hair, which would not stay put under a pinned bonnet. He dismissed her trembling, wavering lower lip and protruding teeth and saw only the love in her heart, the fear in her eyes. He walked with her, patted her arm gently, laughed and talked to her, and listened to her hesitant comments. He even favored her cooking, and he came to her most willing and eager in their marriage bed.

And she had lost him after only four months of marriage. Now she was hired to nurse a young man left to die, now she sat next to a narrow bed and watched a face made beautiful by her longing. She touched the bony hands, wiped the fevered skin, smelled the rising male smell, and thought of her husband, felt the presence of Thomas Miller beside her, and sometimes she even gave in to her despair and buried her face in the covers of the sick bed and cried where no one could hear her.

A wagon had brought the injured man into town, and Martin Smith asked the doctor who he would trust to stay with the patient and nurse him, clean and care for him until the inevitable happened. Dr. Farmer recommended her, Lela Beardsley Miller, as he had on other occasions since the death of her Thomas. It was a poor way to earn a living, but she must do something to keep body and soul together, as Thomas Miller, for all his love and laughter, and his pleasure in their bedtime encounters, had left behind him no buried treasure or small sum to ensure his new wife's continued subsistence.

Mrs. Miller washed her hands after commanding the boy to be more careful in taking out and emptying the chamber pot. She could not abide it when the boy spilled some of the contents and the room stank for hours. She walked back up the stairs and turned down the hall to the small room now occupied by her charge. As she entered the room, she would swear to herself that the stilled body on the bed moved slightly, that the head turned toward the sound of her presence. She knew in her heart, no matter what Dr. Farmer told her, that this young man, called Blue Mitchell, knew when she was near, knew inside his damaged mind that she was there to take care of him.

She also knew, deep inside, that she was romanticizing her patient. He was, in reality, nothing more than an itinerant horse breaker, damaged in his chosen profession, useless now to any rancher, scorned and shoved aside in his infirmity. And he was much too young, twenty years her junior, and too eager still to settle down with only one woman. She had seen him several times in Cimarron, but he had never looked at her, noticed her at all. She could not forget the picture he made on one of Mr. Smith's fine horses. So tall and slender, sitting the horse easily, that blond hair free under his hat, his skin dark from the sun and hard work. And those eyes, those brilliant, unforgettable eyes.

He knew her now, even if he was unconscious and often drugged by the potion Dr. Farmer prescribed. He accepted her hands on him daily, tending to his base needs as well as lovingly washing his face when the fever became too much to bear. She knew his body now, every part of him. She had to be intimate with him, and there were times when she wished most desperately for Thomas to be with her during the nights, so that her hands would not tremble so when she bathed the young man or lifted him onto the chamber pot. She was a strong woman, willing to work hard, and when Mr. Smith offered to hire the boy from the hotel to do the heavy work, she shrugged off the suggestion, unwilling to share even the smallest connection with her patient.

There were times, with her frustration at its peak, when she actually disliked her charge, when her breath came in short gasps and her own face was flushed, and he lay there on the bed, in stark contrast to the white linens that Mr. Smith insisted on purchasing. The hands would lie still, fingers curled and useless, palms pale and no longer calloused. The long legs, the narrow hips, the surprising width of his chest and shoulders when he was stripped of his nightshirt in preparation for his daily bath.

When he lay there, accepting her touch and not responding, and her own body heated and cried out, she hated him with an invigorating intensity.

Today was the thirty-second day Blue Mitchell was left in her care. Lela Miller absently patted his arm and stared blindly at the far wall. She was tired, and discouraged if she allowed herself to think of it. It was true she was well paid, but her patience was beginning to unravel at the sameness of each day, the impossibility of anything new. She so much wanted to see improvement, and yet there was nothing.

A strange noise interrupted her daydreaming. A stirring under the bleached sheet. A hand rose from the bed, the fingers scratched her arm, and she could not shake the memory of her husband's touch. Then Mrs. Miller blinked hard, looked down and stared into the open, blinding eyes of her young man. He abruptly tried to sit up, grabbing her arm for balance and hurting her. She screamed, closed her mouth, and put her hand over it, then screamed again as the hand dug into her flesh and the head wagged sideways, the strange eyes running tears. She could not stop screaming.

The hand dropped away and the body fell back, but the eyes remained open, and Lela Miller could not bring her own gaze away from them. Those beautiful eyes, of the ocean's color, once alive and knowing, now blank and unfocused. Then he spoke, and she was silenced by his voice. The sound was cracked and low, so that she had to lean down to hear him.

As she bent down, the terrible eyes appeared too close, too revealing, and she almost allowed herself to faint from the contact. She wiped her face with both hands, drawing her mouth down, hoping for new strength. The voice began again, and she was just able to make out the words. "Please . . . where am I? Who are . . . why is it dark? Are you there, please . . . touch me. Why is it so dark?"

A voice from the doorway interrupted, and Blue Mitchell's head turned to the new sound. It was the boy from downstairs, the only person in the hotel to answer her screams. "It is all right, Mr. Mitchell is awake now, and he frightened me. I wish you to go right over to Dr. Farmer's, tell him what has happened. It is important he come here immediately. Do you understand?''

She was not certain that the child understood her. There were times when she doubted he understood English or thought he was perhaps retarded. But he nodded, his dark hair falling over his face to hide all expression. And when he turned away and hurried downstairs, Lela Miller chose to believe he would carry out her orders.

Now that she was recovered from her fright, she glanced around the room. True, it was shaded in the room, to place less stress on the invalid, but it was not dark, not like the night could be. Yet he had repeatedly asked why it was so dark.

Then she turned her attention to her patient; his head was rolling side to side endlessly on the pillow, and even though his eyes were thankfully closed, she knew he was awake and fretful. She soothed him like a child, repeating mindless words and patting his hand, stroking his forehead, until the rolling ceased and he lay quietly, once again in a deathless sleep.

Mrs. Miller felt now that her charge would eventually recover. The marks of his fingers on her arm were turning pale blue, as if bruised by his returning strength. But from the evidence of his terrible awakening, she believed that Blue Mitchell was blind.

SIX

THE MAN'S PONDEROUS weight flattened the tired springs
of the old wagon. Even the team of solid horses stepped back
from the pull of the great weight. Albert Buckminster settled
his buttocks on the unpadded seat and rubbed his thigh where
it had hit the top of the iron-rimmed wheel. Someday, very
soon, he would throw away the old wagon and buy a carriage
more suited to his needs, his formidable bulk, and his soon-
to-improve wealth.

It took three slaps of the reins and a strong crack with the
whip before the two horses stepped into their collars and slid
the wagon forward into the street. Buckminster wiped his
face with a grayed kerchief and waved at a friend coming
from the saloon. The friend did not return Buckminster's
greeting, and the big man once again took offense.

Albert Buckminster wore the fat and muscle of a circus
performer, spoke like a reform preacher, and thought like a
successful businessman. The success was confined to his own
impressions, but Buckminster always knew he would eventually be the winner, the best, the man in Cimarron all the
rest admired. Soon enough, in the close future, it would be
he, Albert Buckminster, who accepted waves and calls of
friendship and almost politely nodded his head in amused
condescension.

The wagon springs moaned as the team took a wide corner
at their usual sluggish walk. Buckminster tapped the near

horse, a pale sorrel, with the whip, and the team lurched unevenly into a trot. Buckminster's backside slid on the unplaned board of the seat, and the big man cursed quite violently. He'd been once again assaulted by a digging splinter.

But he would admit the team and wagon, such as they were, meant an improvement over the horses he had ridden almost to death over the years. He was a big man, yes, standing six foot four and weighing more than 250 pounds, and he'd finally grown tired of his mounts' troubles—sore backs, raw mouths, bowed tendons, lameness and coughing, useless. There wasn't a horse in the territory good enough for Albert Buckminster. Even his clothing betrayed him, boots worn through the soles, pants frayed and full of holes, shirts torn at the armpits. Nothing ever buttoned around his neck. By God, Albert Buckminster was more than life-size, and the world wasn't prepared for such magnificence.

Now he drove a poor wagon and a half-dead team, but he'd seen the pair for him, those shiny dark Morgans old Martin Smith owned. And a wagon up to Raton, built special for a company making safes. In a few weeks, maybe a month, Albert Buckminster would arrive in style.

For a man brought into the country twenty years ago to hunt wolf and bear for their pelt and bounty, Albert Buckminster knew he'd come a far distance, and had the rest of his self-inflicted journey close to coming true.

He was a mine owner now, traded the last of his hoarded money three months past for full shares in the big pit he called the Cutheart. That mine was soon going to buy Albert Buckminster back what he'd lost supporting the wrong man.

The mere twinge of that memory squeezed his heart and lungs and brought back the taste of madness. Politics never set right with any free man, and Buckminster still cursed the man's name, still spit on the man's memory. O. P. McMains was the rascal, and his cause was the righteous one of leading the local settlers against the tyranny of the Maxwell Land Grant folks. The loss rankled Buckminster, soured his mouth until he spit twice and coughed into the gray kerchief. O. P. McMains promised those who followed him that it would be

51

their fortune gained in the fight, their prosperity ensured when the land grant was seen for the evil it was.

O. P. McMains, preaching his word and drawing the believers to him. Until the lawyers, the big ranchers, got together and followed Frank Springer into the court system, pushing aside the little folks and winning their right to keep holding on to the land.

Albert Buckminster had gone against his lifetime of independence and stuck with McMains, learned to hate the lawyers and the ranch owners. Learned their names, settled in to despise their lives. Frank Springer and the double-tongued rancher named Martin Smith, those two were the worst.

There wasn't much chance of Buckminster touching on Springer and his clan, his brother and their friends. Latecomers, now powerful, in their prime, the Springers were to be left alone. Martin Smith, old, tired, shaky from his wife's death—now Martin Smith could be real easy to hate, and to be made to pay.

Buckminster lashed out at the slowing team; the whip caught the off horse, a roan mare, above her eye. The mare shied violently, jerked her head, and tried to run against her unwilling partner's short-legged trot. Buckminster laughed; first he'd get his poke from the Cutheart, and then he'd buy up that fine Morgan team, harness them to the wagon bound to be his up in Raton. And then he would drive right up to Smith's front veranda and bang on the door, get that pretty little girl to cling to his arm and go for an evening ride. Just like the quality gentleman Albert Buckminster knew himself to be.

Once past the confines of the main street of Cimarron, Buckminster goaded the team into a ragged gallop. He spread his legs wide, braced his worn boots on the wagon floor, and yelled out his anger, laughed as a hapless bug bounced off his high forehead. The Cutheart would pay out to him, and then he could buy off the bitter memories of the recent past.

Habit made Martin Smith check along the river's edge before he allowed the mare to drink. Then he laughed at himself for the action; there hadn't been Indians or even outlaws to bother him since '76, when the last of the Utes and Jiracillas were driven out. And the final vestige of the land-grant quarrel had disappeared more than a year past, when the country's High Court declared the foreign company's claim on the vast acreage to be valid.

Smith eased himself in the saddle, and the mare paid him no mind. She drank greedily from the cold river. He was a fool, he knew that, at the end of his fading life, all sixty-eight years, and he was still a fool. Spooked into old habits by a river crossing and a few birds flying overhead.

He rubbed both hands against his clean-shaven face. The landmark decision of 1887 drove the impossible Reverend McMains out of Cimarron and ended the long feud. Not much was left, at least not much spilled over from the land grant. Now it was the mines, playing out and quitting, dumping out-of-work and hungry men back on the streets.

It was hard, Martin Smith thought, to really like mankind, when each and every one of them hung their greed on some cause or injustice that served their private purpose while making them out to be selfless and righteous. The Reverend McMain and his followers, they were in the group most definitely. But there were some Martin Smith found difficult to categorize.

Then again, he couldn't not blame himself for his own greed while defiling his neighbors. The land-grant decision gave him full ownership of his land and left him to continue his rich life.

Damn it, Smith thought. His hand reached out and scratched the mare's neck in front of the saddle. Damn it; he'd survived Indian attacks in the fifties, when Cimarron didn't exist, when Rayado was the center of trade. He'd been there to fight for himself and his neighbors when the troops had been pulled out. He'd even lived through Lucien Maxwell and his imperious rule, hot temper, and amazing generosity. It was no wonder the small settlers, seeing the vast expanse of unused land, hated Maxwell. There was no form

53

to the man's decisions, no common sense or practicality. Yet when Maxwell sold to the English lords, there had been well over a million acres of land under his control. It was no small miracle that O. P. McMains and his rabble didn't get their way.

Smith shook his head, caught now in reminiscing; he was a cynic, he supposed, steeped in the mire of human weakness and misery. An old man, one Martin Jerome Smith, closing in to his next birthday. Twice a widower, father of three sons buried on his land, and one daughter young enough to be his own grandchild. The pain of distant memories squeezed him; Smith spurred the mare to cross the river and get going. But he could not outrun his thoughts.

Otis would be fifty now, if he'd lived through the arrow in his chest. And Jerome would have been forty-four yesterday. Jerome, crushed under a spilled wagon at this very crossing of the Cimarron. The third son had not been named; he'd died with his mother on the very day of his birth.

Now Elizabeth, dead six months past, fevered and suffering for more than two years. Her death had been her release, her dying had consigned Martin Smith to Hell.

A wagon was coming down the road too fast. Smith took a firm hold on the chestnut mare's reins; she could take the distraction as an excuse to bolt, and he must be ready. He welcomed the intrusion, wishing to take his thoughts no farther. He had already come to the conclusion that mankind in general was foolish, and in the specific was rarely worth the pain and aggravation of a miserable daily existence.

The chestnut mare tossed her head and showered her rider with strings of water. Unexpectedly Martin Smith laughed and patted the mare's neck again. Horses were his pride and his downfall. This mare was the fourth he had raised from her dam, a blooded filly worthy of her pedigree. It was his conceit, even at his age, to ride a fine horse. But he could not leave his conceit to affect only himself. He could not train his own horses anymore and would not allow a local bronc rider to mistreat and manhandle his pride and joy. No, Martin Jerome Smith could not do anything so ordinary. No,

Martin Smith had to hire a certain young man who came well recommended to work the blooded stock of the Broken S.

Because of his folly, because of his unbending pride, a fine young man lay helpless and mute in a hotel room in Cimarron. Which was why Martin Smith was riding toward town, delaying his journey, attacked by his private devils, and now facing a lunatic in a bouncing wagon headed straight at him.

Because of pride, a good man was maimed and down, and there was nothing left that Martin Smith could do.

Buckminster sawed on the bits, but the team had their minds set to race and did not quickly respond. He could see the single rider ahead, near the crossing of the river, and it was the one man in the territory Albert Buckminster did not want to see.

He knew it was Martin Smith by the fine arch to the horse he sat, the glisten of the chestnut coat, the awkward outline of the old-fashioned saddle, and the shine of silver on the bit and bridle.

Buckminster had a grudge against this man, for his performance in the land-grant quarrel. But it was not yet time to face Smith and rub his haughty nose in Buckminster's impending wealth. It was not yet time. So Buckminster stood up, swayed against the poor balance of the wagon, and drew himself back, hauled on the reins until the team staggered right, skidded from the dirt track, and stumbled into a wide circle on the prairie grasses. The heavy hand on their bridles tore their toughened mouths, and the roan mare stumbled and went to her knees. The old wagon pitched sideways, dragging the near sorrel and Albert Buckminster down in a tangle of harness, splintered wood, and kicking horseflesh.

There were no injuries, other than the rapidly swelling tendon on the sorrel's left front leg. Buckminster rolled and came up on his knees, swore to a godless universe that treated him this badly. The roan mare sat patiently in her collar and traces, while the lamed sorrel stood on three legs. The wagon was shattered, nothing more than kindling for a few winter fires.

And then a man on a high-stepping, glistening chestnut mare came to a halt directly in front of Buckminster as he knelt in the buffalo grass and prairie-dog holes.

"Is there anything I can do for you, Mr. Buckminster? That was a nasty spill, and I think your sorrel has bowed a tendon. Can I help?"

Buckminster roared, shoved his great weight off the ground from his massive wrists, and stood to his full height. His pants were torn down one leg and across the backside, and he could feel the whisper of cold air on bare skin and the prick of tiny cactus. "There ain't nothing you can do, Mr. Smith. No one but the Lord Himself can help me. I will attend to the horses and take care of myself. I ain't bad hurt, if that concerns you. Good day."

The man on his fancy horse looked away from Buckminster, but the big man had seen the smile and felt the impact of the insult. Then the mare was reined back, and horse and rider disappeared. The mare's long tail flowed, her long legs stepped freely, and her arched neck made for a perfect picture. Payment would be due soon, and the punishment would not be swift. Or painless.

When Buckminster remembered to take care of his team, he found the roan mare still sitting patiently, broken reins coiled around her front leg, the bridle hanging from one ear. When Buckminster slapped her on the neck and cursed her, the mare only shook her head and lay down.

When Martin Smith left the chestnut mare at Longacre's Livery, the dour owner already knew why Smith was in town. Doc Farmer was at the hotel right now, Longacre said, tending to the patient and to poor Mrs. Miller. Seems when that cowboy Smith hired sat up and opened his eyes, Mrs. Miller screamed and fainted. Or so Longacre had heard.

Although there was nothing funny in Longacre's morose telling of the news, Martin Smith had to smile. Cimarron was a small town, and everyone knew his neighbor's business.

As he crossed the street, headed toward the St. James, Smith drew a deep breath to steady himself. There had been more to the story than what Longacre retold. Actions, reactions, and consequences still not fully realized that filled out the bare bones of the cowboy sitting up in bed and scaring poor Mrs. Miller until she shrieked and scared the inhabitants of the hotel, even those having their first drink of the day downstairs in the bar.

It had been Peter Charley who reacted first. He saw the stallion and ducked under the fence at the back of the barn and ran. As the stallion reared, he could see the pale underbelly, the head outlined against blue sky. As he ran, he heard the crack of hoof on bone. He had to dodge bewildered ranch hands and discarded gear. The rifle shot did not spook him; as he skidded against the gate of the high corral, he saw the mound of chestnut flesh, smelled the fresh blood, and accepted the necessity of the killing.

As he fumbled with the latch, there was only silence; no one moved, no birds sang or took flight, no horses whinnied, no words passed among the stunned audience.

Inside the pen, Peter Charley found the body rolled up, on the far side of the dead horse. Mitchell's last act, even as he was struck, was to cover his head and belly as he fell. Now he lay as a small child, knees bent to his chest, arms plaited over his wounded head. Peter Charley knelt down, drew in air, and listened to his own breathing before he placed his fingers on Mitchell's skull, on the tender place beneath the jaw where life ran close to the surface. He pressed deeply, felt nothing. Waited a moment, expelled pent-in air, pressed his fingers to that spot again.

Blood moved against his flesh; Blue Mitchell was alive. Peter Charley began his practical examination. The blond hair was matted with blood, the shirt stained, the ground spattered with red. He quickly ran his hands along the arms and legs, touched the ribs, felt the neck. Then he gently loosened the clothing near the arms and legs and rolled the man over to lie on his back. The slack mouth moved slightly, and a faint groan escaped. Peter Charley rolled the head sideways and saw the wound. The left temple was nearly split by the striking hoof, the wound was slightly swollen, and there was little fresh blood. The bleeding had stopped of itself. Peter Charley did not know if that was a good sign.

Movement near his left side did not startle Peter Charley. It was the girl, Miss Flora. Peter Charley cursed silently whatever had brought her into the corral. She would cry and whimper and take the intent away from the injured man, place it on her own foolish needs. Peter Charley saw no beauty or sweetness in this child; he saw only temper and selfishness.

She confounded his judgment of her by settling into place near his left elbow and offering torn material to wipe off the blood. She did not scream; she did not screw up her face in pantomimed disgust. She wanted only to know if the man was alive, and then how badly injured. There was no way yet to know, Peter Charley told her. No certainty about the blow's effect.

As he spoke, he could again hear the sharp crack of hoof on bone, and the echo disturbed him. He wondered if the girl could hear that sound.

There were more people in the corral, silent, eyes asking and uncertain. He told them to bring a door, told Miss Flora to get her father, get a bed ready inside the house, boil water, tear more cloths.

The ministrations were simple and quickly done after Mitchell was gently carried inside on the door. The cut was first bathed, allowed to bleed again to flush out any remaining corral dirt. A bandage was tied lightly over the raw cut, and then the unconscious man was allowed to lie in darkness, in peace. Peter Charley sat with him. A bruise slowly appeared, showing dark around the edge of the white bandage. A vein throbbed unevenly across the new coloring.

As father and daughter discussed what was to be done, Peter Charley went about his chores. It took the team of

Morgans and much urging before the dead animal was pulled out of the corral and dragged a half mile out on the grassland. There the coyotes would eat well, and the ravens would caw their satiated delight. There no one would have to witness and remember. Peter Charley turned the team out in the offending pen, where they snorted and trotted the confines as if still in harness. Finally tiring of the game, they walked to the piles of hay the Indian had put down for them.

After several hours of the patient showing no signs of consciousness, it was decided to take him to town. Martin Smith ordered the team harnessed, the wagon readied. Mitchell was still alive, he said, but he had not stirred, and it was best to take him in to be under a doctor's care.

When the long body was laid gently on the padded wagon bed, Peter Charley touched his fingers again to the skull, above the stained bandage. There was a soft indentation in the bone. He put a finger to each eyelid and raised it, stared again at the wild-colored eyes. The dark center was fixed; the whites bled with internal blood. That there was life in the stilled body became a small miracle. Peter Charley climbed in the wagon seat and clucked to the patient team.

As he made his wide circle toward the road, he was not surprised when the boss rode ahead on his fine chestnut mare. And he again was not surprised when Martin Smith whipped the mare into a gallop along the bend of the river, through the crossing and out of sight. The man would try to outride his new sadness. Peter Charley had worked for the man five long years. He knew the man. The life or death of Blue Mitchell would weigh on Martin Smith. Peter Charley drove the team steadily, at a walk where the track was rough, at a slow trot when it would not disturb his uncomplaining passenger.

For himself, Peter Charley preferred to be alone. White men eyed his color, his eyes, and the shape of his face, and they laid their anger on him. An Indian might work a white man's way, but he lived in safety only when he was alone. His companion on this drive was not inclined to talk, and Peter Charley valued the silence.

The rear wheel hit a rut because the driver had to scratch his neck and the off horse took a notion to shy. The body laid out on the blankets groaned and sat up, crying as if the devil were inside him. Peter Charley hauled up the spooked team roughly, frightened himself for what was happening. He looked behind him, and an involuntary cry came from him. The blond hair covered the bandaged face, and the bony hands pawed at the entangled strands. But the sightless eyes were opened, the mouth loosened, and strings of saliva hung from the lips.

Peter Charley shook as he climbed over the wagon seat and knelt beside the man. He grabbed for the restless hands and held them, talked in his own tongue as if Blue Mitchell could understand. The eyes remained open, the hair shoved back; there was no life in the stare, no recognition. The hands abruptly stopped their struggle, the head drooped, and the body became limp, a weight far too heavy for Peter Charley to hold. He laid the stilled body back on its rumpled bed and waited until he was certain nothing more would happen. And he prayed as he climbed back over into the wagon seat, picked up the reins, and guided the team into a slow trot. He prayed to the Christian god of his formal schooling and to the remembered gods of his family. Blue Mitchell would come back to life; for this Peter Charley prayed. But for now, Blue Mitchell was close to dead.

By the time he reached Cimarron with his burden, Martin Smith had made the arrangements. Several unnamed men crowded around the wagon when Peter Charley stopped in front of the St. James Hotel, where Smith's mare stood tied to the rail. Peter Charley carried the shoulders of the injured man, and they made a poor procession through the fine lobby of the hotel and up the carpeted stairs to the second floor. Peter Charley had not been inside the hotel; he was an Indian and was not allowed in such places.

A bed was readied in a small room, its covers turned back, its pillows plumped and waiting to receive the shattered head of the horse tamer. Charley was the one to position the head on those pillows; they would suffocate the man with their intentions. Herbs were needed, and prayers, and a darkened place for sleep, fresh air, water. Not lights, voices, and closed windows, heavy blankets and too many people watching and whispering.

A large woman stood inside the room, a woman judged homely by the townspeople. Peter Charley had heard of her and now understood the gossip. He shook his head, and for a moment it was as if the woman understood. Then she let her gaze drift from Peter Charley and her face flushed, her eyes blinking rapidly. He had seen this before, a white woman shocked at her first glimpse of an Indian.

There was nothing more; Peter Charley put his hand on the damp face of Blue Mitchell. It was not good, none of this was good; the fever burned his skin, and he removed his hand. He was hurried outside by the stifling presence of too many curious people and the strong smells of uncleanliness. The smells of white men living close together. It was not good.

Dr. Horace Farmer had the onlookers removed from the room; only he and Martin Smith and the big, awkward woman were left. He examined Blue Mitchell and told Smith exactly what he found. That the young man had a cracked skull, a bad concussion. He showed few signs of life other than an unsteady pulse and a rising fever. All that could be done now was to keep him warm and quiet, bathe his face when the fever was too much, tend to his bodily needs, and wait.

The doctor's orders had been given a month past, after the terrible accident and Peter Charley bringing the injured man into Cimarron. There had been no change, no improvement, no deterioration.

Now the summons came to Martin Smith that his horse tamer had spoken some gibberish and opened his eyes and then collapsed, after scaring his nurse half to death. Even old Longacre knew more than Martin Smith did about the occurrences.

Flashes of that day walked with Martin Smith as he crossed the wide street from the livery and turned to the hotel. He did not want more death on his conscience; he did not believe he could stand the implications, the addition to his long list of mortal sins.

He hastened when he recognized Dr. Farmer at the door of the St. James. Now perhaps there would be good news, something positive that would take away the bitter taste of all those deaths in his past. Otis, Jerome, the unnamed son. His wife Elizabeth.

Perhaps, after all, Blue Mitchell would live.

SEVEN

THE ROAD INTO Cimarron was fine for a wagon or a horse, or a stagecoach with six cart horses to pull it. But for walking, the road was unpassable. Any road would be more than useless. Especially for a big man in broken-down boots, who was forced to lead one reluctant mare and a goddamned lamed gelding, because neither horse had a back comfortable enough for a man to sit on and not effectively geld himself on a protruding bone.

Albert Buckminster hated to walk, but he hated more the picture of himself riding the sorry roan mare in a blinkered bridle and knotted reins while threatening the miserable gelding at each step with a long, flexible tree branch. Even the damned whip had been torn apart in the accident. Snapped off in Buckminster's hands as he attempted to get the mare on her feet.

He left behind him a dismantled wagon, piles of harness rotted in places where it had not already been torn or busted. He led the two horses only because he knew there was a price waiting for the lamed gelding for the tallow and hide, not to mention a few rump steaks cooked and served to unsuspecting diners in the local eatery. Not the St. James, no sir, Henri Lambert, he would not stoop to serving up stringy horse meat to his customers, but in the other place in town, the owner had no such scruples.

At least it meant that Buckminster could eat for a few days

while he tried to figure out his revenge on Martin Smith and waited for the return on his major mining investment.

He didn't have a twinge of conscience as the sorry gelding limped and bobbed its head at each stride. He didn't wince when he blamed all the damned misfortune on Martin Smith. Smith had been the cause of the destruction; Smith had best pay out. No one else in the sorry town of Cimarron would reimburse Albert Buckminster what was owed him.

When he finally reached Longacre's Livery, the hostler refused to take in the sorry gelding and the roan mare. "Owe me too much back board, you do, Buckminster. Ain't paid a bill in two weeks, and word's out on your mine. I ain't taking in those nags for nothing."

There was no justice in the short speech; Buckminster clenched his hands and thought how quickly they could wrap around the old man's neck and squeeze until . . . then he caught the meaning from the old man's words. Something about a mine, his mine. What word? He wanted to confront the hostler and shake the truth from him, but he had to keep hold of the two horses. The roan mare showed signs of wanting to sit down again, and the sorrel's head drooped, his front hoof barely touching the ground.

It was time now to deal with the horses. He would return and deal with the sour old man later. Much later, when there weren't so goddamn many people sitting around, watching, looking, thinking their own pure thoughts and calling judgment in on Albert Buckminster.

He puffed himself up, spoke out in his best voice, not giving in to the pressure put on him so unjustly. "Sir, I am sorry the bill slipped my mind. I will deal with these two nags and return to make restitution. Good day, sir." The hostler barely turned his head at the speech, and spit into a steaming pile of manure and straw, expressing his feelings about Albert Buckminster and his word.

Cool air tantalized him, drifting in small bursts over his face, teasing him with the scent of flowers and grass, dust and manure, green trees and cold water. Then soft hands cradled his head as he tried to sit up and turn toward the breath of air. The hands restricted him, smoothed back his damp hair, and held his shoulders until he could no longer fight their impersonal support and had to lie back in the bed.

He didn't know where he was or what had happened; he couldn't understand why it was always dark. No cracks showed around a door frame; no evening light came through an open window. He knew there was a window; he could feel the life-giving air. But it was pitch-black always, as dark as he had ever seen the night. He was scared, terrified of his suspicions, and no one would explain what had happened, no one would tell him about the darkness. There were soft hands and gentle voices, but no one would answer his unspoken question.

Blue rolled his head on the damp pillow and heard the moan, hated himself for the weak sound. His right hand worked free of an unseen restraint, and he touched his face in hope. There were no bandages or pads taped over his eyes. He bit back a new groan, deep from his heart. His trembling hand brushed the bare hollow of his eyelids, and he knew there was no reason for the dark.

His body arched, his legs stiffened, and his shoulders pressed against the trap of the featherbed. He groaned, the sound rising to a wild sob, and his strength quit him. His body dropped back into the bed, his head rolled sideways, and he could feel the betraying tears even though he could not see them.

Hands gripped his wrists; he fought, but he could not get free. He spit curses, yet the hands did not let go. Exhaustion slowed him, a new fever swamped him, and he slid between unconsciousness and sleep.

Lela Miller had to sit down. Her own hands, banded with red marks against their whiteness, trembled badly as she pressed them together. Her heart pounded, and dots swam in front of her eyes. He had come back to life against the doctor's prediction; he was alive, and blind.

Supposedly Mr. Smith was on his way in from the Broken S, in response to the earlier awakening, and her scream of terror upon seeing a corpse sit up, realizing the young man was blinded.

This time there had been no one around to witness Blue Mitchell's erratic behavior; this time only she was there, to comfort him and hold him until he once again could sleep.

She was glad for his need to sleep; she did not know how to answer that one terrible question. How could she say to a cowboy, a young man who lived his life by his hands, his manual skills, that he was blind.

As she sat and tried to understand, her patient groaned again, and she jumped, fearful he would become excited and perhaps injure himself. She worried as he twisted and rolled in the small bed, arms almost freed of the tucked sheet, wet hair plaited from the endlessly rolling head. She put her cool hand on his forehead, touching gently, putting her heart into the comforting gesture, and the endless rolling side to side abruptly ceased. Glancing toward the door, Lela Miller leaned down and so softly kissed the damp skin next to the drawn mouth. The taste was sweet, of sweat and her soap and water and the basic aroma of a male.

Diaz scrubbed vegetables and peeled potatoes for the kitchen at the St. James, as well as running errands for the big señora who made him empty the stinking pot and take out the soiled bed clothes for the sick gringo. Within these tasks, and aided by his refusal to look anyone in the eye and his lack of apparent courage, Diaz managed to exist.

He lived in back of the hotel, in an odd structure nailed to three cottonwoods that shaded the hotel kitchen. He had managed a discarded tarpaulin for a roof and even had a torn rug to make a floor. It was much better than many places where he had lived, so Diaz was willing to endure a certain amount of humiliation from the hotel and its people.

Such privacy was a novelty; Diaz had grown to his eighteen years in crowded hovels and stable yards, alternatively abused and forgotten. He was not much to look at and did not long remain in anyone's memory; thin, short, black hair, and traitorous Indian features mocked by light blue eyes and freckles. He was truly not worthy of being remembered.

And Cimarron was little different; here the owner of the hotel did not actually speak to Diaz, but he allowed the raw-boned child to work in the back kitchen and eat his fill, and even be paid in coin for extra work. Such as doing the ugly señora's bidding.

Thus Henri Lambert and his fine establishment earned Diaz's gratitude, while Mrs. Miller was worthy only of scorn and pranks. That was, until he began to work for her when she lived in the hotel and cared for the injured man. She was firm with Diaz, and yet tender to him, asking if he ate enough, how he slept. Common courtesies among gentle folk, courtesies that escaped most of Diaz's life.

He had later come to worship Mrs. Miller, anticipating his daily routine of emptying the chamber pot, an odorous job that he no longer minded. She would ask how he was, she would talk of small incidents that pleased her, she would smile and push back the dark hair that hung in his eyes and tell him she hoped he was taking care, doing his work, listening to his betters, and accepting responsibility. Most of the time Diaz did not fully understand what it was she meant, but he loved the sound of the words and the sweetness in her eyes when she spoke to him. Her face, which he had once thought ugly, had become dear to him, special in a way he did not wish to examine.

Now the injured man had come back to life; now she spoke only of that miracle and did not bother with Diaz, did not worry about his health or question him on his work. What rose in Diaz now was confusion fed by anger and jealousy. Hatred for a man almost dead, who could not see and still could not sit up and feed himself. He must be hand-fed by the señora, his face and body intimately bathed by her. It was this that disturbed Diaz and made him stumble when he carried the stinking pan from the room. He would wish he had emptied its contents on the sleeping man, but for her worried glance.

As much as Diaz did not want to know this, he could not

truly hate a man who lay on a dying bed, between sleep and death, fighting for life. So much lost time, so much sadness; truly it was impossible to hate such a man, but the temptation was there in Diaz's soul.

Instead, as he carried out the fouled pan, he carried it down the front stairs of the hotel, an act of defiance, an act meant to push the boundaries of the man who stood at the landing, deep in thought, staring out the window that Diaz washed each week. It was the man who owned the killing horse, the man who paid dear Mrs. Miller to tend his victim. A small act of defiance, to be sure, and one Diaz would not consider except that he knew Henri Lambert was not in the hotel, not even in the town of Cimarron.

He grinned widely and risked looking into the old man's eyes as he passed him on the landing above the stairs. And when the man was so rude as to turn his face away and wrinkle his nose at the smell, Diaz nodded a friendly greeting, as if they were *compadres*, as if he carried nothing more than a bunch of flowers for a kind lady.

It was a small act of revenge, but its boldness pleased Diaz, and he managed the stairs without tripping. When he reached the bottom and looked back, he saw Señor Smith wiping his face, blowing out hard snorts of air, as if the passage of that mortal odor offended him. Diaz was content and went out the side door to empty the pan and return to his kitchen duties.

He was impatient for Doc Farmer to get upstairs. So he stopped at the landing, stared out the window, and saw the bulk of Albert Buckminster leading his two disreputable horses toward Longacre's Livery. Martin was glad he would not hear that exchange; Longacre would not hold his tongue, and Buckminster had the sense of a flea-ridden bear.

Where was Farmer? He'd said he'd be right along, that there was a small matter he needed to attend to first, in the bar. Martin Smith blew through his nose like a gun-shy bronc. A small matter.

The air turned foul, and he glanced in back of him; the

kid Henri Lambert had do small chores was advancing, carrying a familiar item teeming with its unholy contents. If Martin was less charitable, he would have called the look on the strange, mismatched face one of triumph and glee.

He snorted again, dispelling the overwhelming smell. Annoyed now, both at Farmer and the foolish errand boy, Martin Smith held his ground only out of duty to the injured man.

The word had been garbled, confused, enticing as it said Mitchell had come back to life, frightening in the implication the man could not see.

To hell with it all; Martin Smith stared out the window and saw Buckminster yank on the bridle reins of his two miserable horses. Longacre's shape was gone inside his stable. Buckminster hobbled down the road stabbing his heavy feet into the offending dirt.

He wanted the years of feuding and hatred to end. Smith sighed deeply at the unbidden thought. With the mines going, talk of a railroad coming to Cimarron, ranching in a spiral of prosperity, such imaginings had seemed possible. Now, again, not for the first time, it was going to hell fast. Mines were playing out, talk was back and forth about irrigation while the range land dried up from nature's annual rain shortage. And the railroad; more fool's talk.

Peace in the small community had no chance. Martin Smith saw the plain picture of Albert Buckminster and knew that truth. He gripped the edge of the window frame with both hands. Fools were incarnate in the lumpish, loudmouth, ignorant form of Buckminster. One who embodied the worst, from an ugly face and form to poor manners and an illiterate, greedy mind.

Martin's hands ached; he stared at them and saw the veins pump his sluggish blood across the liver-spotted flesh. Old age, by God, swollen joints and stiff muscles, bones tired from hard work, with only more ahead of him before he too died.

He was thankful for the interruption of the woman's voice. Self-pity was not a charming trait in any man. And then he could hear Horace Farmer's loud voice echo out of the St. James Hotel bar.

They were needed to tend the patient; the drunken doctor, the weak-minded rancher, and the homely woman. She would be calm and quiet, asking politely, never complaining. Good lord, but she was homely; old Miller had to have been a saint to buy and bed the woman. He had a flash of Miller, bandy-legged and short, smiling, joking, full of life. And then Martin Smith stared into the window's crude glass and saw himself—pinched face, balding, bent with his years. Certainly no beauty. What judgments mankind laid upon others and yet rarely on themselves.

Mrs. Miller's polite voice called to him again, and he heeded her unspoken command. Horace Farmer's footsteps sounded on the worn carpet; the troops were forming to tend the enemy. He barked a short laugh, and Doc Farmer stared up as if personally insulted.

Before he went with the rum-soaked doctor, Smith saw out the landing window one more time and was rewarded with the sight of Buckminster's form slamming between two doors into the Miner's Saloon.

The figures tallied out when he sat down at the table and worked them with a pencil and the ends of his fingers. Spud Morgan sat across from him with both hands wrapped around a mug of beer. Morgan wasn't bright enough to tell more than the truth, and as he worked out the numbers, Buckminster could see how deep in trouble he was.

The Cutheart Mine was played out, busted. Buckminster pushed the paper aside and swallowed the last of his beer. The bitterness suited him. Morgan laughed, and Buckminster looked up, ready to take offense. But it was a drunk sprawled in a corner chair, hawking stupid, rambling words. Morgan took his time to focus in on Buckminster, first finishing the beer and wiping foam on the back of his grimy hand.

"Well now, Buck, that mine gave us a run. Told you when you come in asking for shares she was as worn out as a forty-year whore. You stand there giving me big words and offer more working cash, hell, mister, I ain't man 'nough to turn you down.'' Morgan signaled for more beer, and Buckminster tapped his pocket out of habit. Morgan grinned at him. "Hell, Buck, I can spend out my own coin on beer. You drink up with me, nothing left but to drink and blow out the goddamned lights and find another mine. Been doing it most of my life. Guess I ain't bright 'nough to do different now.''

Buckminster stared at the man who'd been his short-term partner. Spud Morgan's face was a series of black lines, his head egg-bald and his eyes walleyed and shiny. Buckminster wondered if it was the cockeyed looking that kept Morgan content with that damned smile of his.

Then he decided it made no difference; a pitcher of beer sat on their table, and Morgan poured it out evenly. Morgan drank hard, wiped his wet whiskers on a filthy shirt sleeve, belched, and spit on the sawdust floor. Albert Buckminster copied the moves but was disgusted with himself. This wasn't why he'd come west twenty years ago, making money off of wolf hides and bear skins, deer and buffalo meat if he could find them. He'd gotten smart fast, investing in horse herds to mount the army going to come to the unofficial Fort Rayado.

But the fort never got its vital recognition, and Buckminster's horses were sold off cheap; now his mine, once thought to be endless, was coming up empty like the Aztec and the Montezuma, and even the French Henry. Barely producing enough to pay a miner's wage.

That wasn't how Buckminster meant to make his fortune. He slammed his hands down on the table and watched the pitcher rock. Morgan easily swiped the pitcher, poured the last of the beer into his glass, and raised it in mock salute to his partner's fury.

"By God, Buck, I'll drink the last of this-here stuff and get back to working in that hellhole you folks down here call Elizabethtown. By God, we may be going broke, but the day is glorious and the world's a fine place. Lot more mines for me to dig in, lot more.''

Morgan finished the beer, and Buckminster watched him,

71

no longer spilling over with his anger. It wasn't the fool's fault, that news from the mine. It was square placed on Martin Smith and the Springer brothers, who'd been bragging over the local mines at the hotel one night. They were the ones, they'd gone on about the possibility of great riches in the Cimarron area. That blame didn't belong to a black-seamed, walleyed son who laughed and called Buckminster "partner" no longer.

He ordered himself a pitcher of beer and watched the miners, now filled with whiskey and beer and pickled eggs, pick up their blackened hats and wipe their smudged eyes. Time to get to the next vein, time to break their backs and their dreams hammering at another man's gold.

The beer was warm and stale. Its weak foam brushed Buckminster's nose and stung the inside of his belly. He sipped mindlessly, intent on his bleak thoughts, heedless of faces watching him. Word would get around that the Cutheart was petered out; word would flourish that Albert Buckminster was broke again. That particular word would please one Martin Smith. The man would gloat on his rival's bad luck, calling it poor judgment rather than what it truly was. Luck, pure bad luck. The thought soured the beer in him, turned his eyes blank and mean, raised the spiral of his loose temper.

Smith and Springer, both of them, not asking Buckminster to join their visionary causes, not thinking enough of his talents to choose his company. He could hate these men; they saw only his bulk and heard his rough tongue and knew his reputation as a wolfer. Hellfire, Smith himself had been a wolfer once. Smith and his kind, the Springer brothers, they judged him a failure, a lout not grand enough to join their exalted ranks.

He rolled his numbed tongue around the edge of his teeth. A back molar ached when he touched it. He winced, brushed his hands on his jaw, and felt the rasp of two-day-old whiskers. So he was not the best-groomed figure, so he wore the vestiges of his old trade. Those facts did not rule out his

72

brain or his schemes; those facts did not make the Springers and Martin Smith easily his superiors.

He would plan carefully and wait his time, and Martin Smith would be beaten. It would not be long before Albert Percy Buckminster shed his wolf clothing and walked through town resplendent in broadcloth and top hat, wearing fine leather boots and carrying a hand-carved cane.

Then Martin Smith would invite the conqueror into his home.

Then Frank and Charles Springer would bow and listen.

The dream was strong, and the beer tasted like fine whiskey. Buckminster leaned back in the complaining chair and closed his eyes to enjoy the dream.

EIGHT

HIS LEGS WORKED. They ached, and his bare feet were cold, but he could bend the legs at the knee joint and even slide them across the bed and plant his feet on the wooden floor.

His hands worked, too, but they were slow. His fingers were thick, numb, his wrists stiff and his elbows hurt to flex or try and move his shoulders. As if a great weight had slammed into him and left his entire body bruised.

At first he made a game of lifting each finger, counting numbers as the tips touched the scratchy blanket. The middle finger of his left hand was the toughest; a bay mare had half bitten it off two years ago, he thought he remembered that much.

He struggled with the slightest movement of his hands and feet and fought the dizziness that sitting up brought on. He had to focus on a daily improvement because he couldn't see, couldn't see anything at all.

He didn't know what day it was or how he'd been injured. He knew the room was stuffy, that he was often too hot, but when he pulled the covers off, a firm voice said he was naughty, and strong hands held him down, tucked the imprisoning covers around him again. He knew the voice and hands belonged to a woman, by the smell of the air near him, by the touch, by the smooth feel of the large palm. The voice came in a whisper, as if afraid to startle him by lifelike sound. But he knew his caretaker was a woman.

He wondered often about her, how she must react during the worst of his sickness, when she had to clean and bathe him. He was thankful his eyes were darkened then, so he could not see her face or be responsible for his own red-faced embarrassment.

No one but a woman would use the word "naughty" in connection with him. It was almost funny to think on it. Wild, yes; a hell-raiser, a bastard son of a bitch was what his uncle called him. Bad pure through was the old man's favorite, said most often when he'd been hired out to work and got sent back for raising too much hell, speaking out his mind.

The memories did Blue no good, lying in the enforced dark, smelling his sour odor, at the mercy of his own weakness. He lay there too long and thought too much. A beating usually came with each return to the small cabin in the cold valley, a harsh beating and then a new job at a new place, with words said to the boss that "the poor stupid son of a bitch don't know no better; you got to beat him to keep him in line." Some of the bosses did just that; some looked on the child with compassion and treated him as if he was human.

But he'd left that old man years past, left the cold valley and the high winter snows and ridden south, into Utah and then Arizona and on toward New Mexico. There were images of horses, a roan outlaw who tried to tear him apart, mixed in with signals of a rearing stallion.

Here his mind quit him and Blue panicked, fought the tight sheets binding him, struggled for his freedom.

Lela Miller's big hand unconsciously patted the frayed edges of her hair, trying to neaten her appearance. She stood up, tugged at her collar, and pushed her escaping shirtwaist deeper into the band of her worn skirt. Martin Smith's steps were on the front stairs of the St. James. He was about to visit his ward for the third time since the young man had surfaced from unconsciousness.

And of course there was Diaz again, carrying the once-white chamber pot high, almost proudly. Right past Mr. Smith as he turned the last step to mount the landing. She could imagine that Mr. Smith's face visibly whitened from the appalling stench and that his face turned automatically toward the view out the landing window rather than look past Diaz and see Lela Miller herself.

So Mrs. Miller stood in the opened sickroom door and contented herself with waiting. She knew her appearance was vaguely foolish, a big, awkward woman too homely for such as Martin Smith to notice. She contented herself with watching the gentleman's back as he stared out the window and ignored Diaz's trip down the carpeted stairs.

A noise from the bed disturbed her; she glanced at her patient, but he was sleeping again, worn out from the brief struggle of a few minutes past. How thin he was, a long shape barely noticeable in the narrow bed. Quieted now, feverish again, but snoring slightly, a commonplace sound that reassured her. He did not wince when he was awake and she spoke to him; he did not look away from her homely face and misshapen body. No distaste or bad humor marred those intriguing features when his head rotated toward her voice. He was blind, he could not be offended by her.

Last evening, on the verge of climbing into her own bed, she found a terrible thought lodged inside her—she hoped he would stay blind. For her sake only, to give her one human who would not run from her approach. The thought had snuck up on her, a most unchristian, sinful thought, but it intruded while she dozed in the chair near her patient's bed or when she bathed him, or even, God help her, when she placed him on the pan for his toilet. The act embarrassed her and humiliated him, but she could no more banish it from her mind than she could make herself beautiful by combing out her hair differently or binding her clumsy body in whalebone corsets and padding it with ornamental cloth.

Blue Mitchell accepted her ministrations, her expression

of love, and he did not wince at the sight of her or turn away from the sound of her voice, unlike Mr. Martin Smith, and even the two Springer brothers. They were polite, gracious, but they did not ever truly see the Lela Miller who existed trapped inside the ugliness of her mortal form.

Mr. Smith had still not appeared in the room. With a quick glance to reaffirm that the young man slept peacefully, Lela Miller stepped out into the hall. She had gotten only a few steps beyond the door when she heard the crash, and then the screaming started. Loud enough to wake the dead from Trinidad to Clayton. Lela Miller jumped, and the fine painting Lambert had hanging from the wall rattled and threatened to fall. Lela's hands fluttered around her throat, and her mouth opened for an instinctive answering cry. The scream intensified, and Lela Miller began to sob.

It was Martin Smith who grabbed her arm and spun her around. "For God's sake, woman, help him." Smith pulled her toward the room and dragged her inside. The dark room was suddenly very crowded. Mitchell was on the floor, rolled on his side, arms flailing, nightshirt bunched at his waist. He scrambled at their entry, came to his knees, and drew back his arms, both fists ready to strike. His eyes were wide open, and Lela Miller began crying again. The blue of those eyes hurt; blind, unseeing, terrorized.

Her patient was a madman; foam smeared his mouth, and the long hair was twisted around his skull. He shook, rocked back and forth on his knees, ready to fight what he could not see. Martin Smith stepped to the left, between Mitchell and the window, and even though the eyes could not focus, the head followed the sound of Smith's footsteps.

Lela Miller drew a sharp breath as one of Mitchell's arms caught Martin Smith. Smith did not pull back as the hand tore his sleeve, scratched his skin. Smith grabbed for the other hand, and the screaming started again. Smith drew back his own clenched fist and hit Mitchell's jaw hard. The solid sound rocked in Lela Miller's head; her patient crumpled onto the dim floral rug.

Together they were able to put young Mitchell back in the

77

bed. Smith kept one hand on the bony chest when Mitchell tried to resist, and it was odd to watch the aging, almost frail rancher so easily dominate the much younger man. Mr. Smith kept his hand on Mitchell, even after Mitchell was laid out the length of the bed. A sigh came from Mitchell's drawn lips, and his body finally collapsed on itself, offering no more fight.

Lela Miller busied herself with tucking in the sheets, drawing them tight across the body to form a barrier with which to keep him quiet. When she finished her ministrations and straightened up, put two hands to the small of her back, Martin Smith met her gaze across the bed. There was no disgust in the man this time; he nodded at their good work, motioned to the sick young man, and silently thanked her for her help. There was little need or urge to speak. They shared a bond of sympathy newly forged. Lela Miller looked down one more time at Blue Mitchell and sighed. Martin Smith sighed with her and then quietly left the dismal room.

She stared into the mirror, displeased with what she saw. According to her father, her hair was exactly the color of her mother's, the color when her mother was young and sweet and courted by her father, who was almost thirty years older than the girl he took for his second bride. This her father told her often, when he was moved to talk at length about his dear Elizabeth; as if Flora, their child, was alive only to be a memory of the mother, not to be a woman of her own.

The thick hair was a soft brown highlighted with red. Auburn, her mother called it; sunset was how her father chose to describe its color. Sunset, as if her mother had been a fleeting color, a short time of day, and not a human being at all.

It was how Flora imagined herself through her father's sad eyes; a model child framed by the wings of her mother's favorite chair. Perfect in a flowery dress chosen by her mother's eye, wrapped in a shawl of her mother's design. For her father to watch and worship now, then tuck back into a box until she was needed again to ease his terrible loneliness.

There was no room in all of this for Flora's own loneliness, her isolation from friends her own age, her need for an older woman to explain everything to her. Unless the tears and the whiskey weakened her father and he sat and talked with her, admired her, told her how much she reminded him of his Elizabeth, there was no one to talk to, no one to play with. And Flora was not a dull or stupid child, despite her early frailty, her childhood illnesses.

She pulled several pins from the hair piled on her head and let the long strands flow freely. Beautiful hair, her father said; please pin it this way, just like the photograph taken of your dear mother two weeks before we were married in Kansas. Please, her father said. Please. It is soothing for me, and you are so beautiful, so much like your mother.

Despite her father, she was not dulled by her endless childhood sickness nor the long wasting that had taken her mother. She had not grown up blind to the succession of cowboys and their talk, the repeated spring prancings of the fine English thoroughbred stallions. She knew how a bull mounted a cow; she had watched a randy horse court and skewer a frightened filly. Flora rubbed her face with two damp hands. Her imagination was fueled daily with procreation, yet she was expected to blush and shy away from such approaches by any young men of her father's distant approval. She was expected to simper behind closed hands at a man's casual touch; she was meant to stay helpless and bound within her own rising passion.

Flora's mouth opened slightly, and she was conscious of the tenderness of her flesh. Her father was sometimes a fool, never thinking of his daughter's growing up. He eased himself with a ride into Cimarron, to be released by a female's paid touch, and left behind unthinkingly a grown-up child alone in the company of rough cowhands and her own imagination.

That Blue Mitchell began to intrigue her was her father's fault. It was at his request that she sat with him on the veranda and watched Mitchell work the horses, calm and playful with the filly until she was willing to be saddled and ridden. By the time Mitchell had begun the rest of the blooded stock, Flora Smith had made up her mind.

And then there came the terrible accident. It was most definitely her father's fault, with his insistence that she watch this particular man and learn from his every move. It wasn't that Blue was good-looking, not in the refined, well-mannered way of the acceptable townsmen. It was the long hands and those remarkable eyes, the gentle voice with a surprising humor in it, when he chose to speak to her.

Flora well knew the unspoken law that separated the bunkhouse from the main house. But that separation did not extend to an injury, especially one as serious as that which had brought down Blue Mitchell. It was well within her duties as her father's daughter to become his nurse here at the ranch, now that he was beginning to recover.

She wondered sometimes, when alone, watching the horses, thinking and bored with nothing much to do. She wondered if Blue's parents had named him well, or had he been called by a nickname so long he could not remember his given name. It came from the eyes, she knew that; any fool could guess that one. She had certainly not met one quite like Blue. Scarred by his chosen profession, he remained a free soul, choosing and rejecting who paid him by whim or distraction. He stood alone, the possessor of a talent that allowed him freedom. It was in his hands and in the laughter of those wonderful, deep eyes.

If she were forced into the truth, Flora would say that Blue Mitchell had not crossed the line, had not sought her out or pursued her or attempted any unseemly behavior. The pursuit had come from Flora, the chase had originated from her curiosity and her knowledge, and her incomplete loneliness.

It was impossible to be what her father wished for her—a poised, frozen virgin who waited only for a ghost to love her. She would have the same release bought by her father on his rides into Cimarron. She would have passion and desire mixed with a child's frivolity. She chose Blue Mitchell and she chose well. For there was a quiet reserve and a sense of honor in him that would unwittingly keep her safe.

She was the one. She had kissed him and pressed herself against him and felt the hard core of his body and loved the new sensation. She had not kissed a man before; she had been kissed only by her father. The forbidden taste of his mouth was new and exciting.

Now he was injured, recovering, her father said. She was newly determined to bring him home, cherish his renewed strength, play with him until she learned the function of a man in a woman's life. She would bring him back into what would be his home, she would bathe him and caress him, tend to him and love him until he belonged only to her.

NINE

Smith came out of the St. James Hotel, and he was not alone. It weren't that drunken doc with him neither. Hell, his tongue was so thick he could brush it. Lost all that educated sound he'd worked on, hell, again it didn't matter. No one listened to him nohow.

But it was Smith and one of the Springers standing on the hotel steps and talking at each other. Buying up more land, most likely, taking away more of Buckminster's chance to win. He'd been planning after the next two ore shipments was sent out and bought up, he was planning or had been planning to buy land. Good land along the river, more land up by Ponil Creek, any land still setting and ready to sell.

And then those two, standing there mouthing off at each other, they'd have the cash in their bulging pockets and they'd buy what rightly belonged to Albert Buckminster and lost 'cause of that damned played-out Cutheart Mine.

Weren't Buckminster's fault, not his fault. Belonged to other men, tempting him to buy shares in a near-worthless mine, taking his cash off good land to buy disappearing gold. Weren't Buckminster's fault at all.

Smith was in visiting that dumb wrangler who got kicked in the head. Buckminster rubbed where he guessed the wound had been. Poor dumb son of a bitch, sure tell he wouldn't get paid much by Smith to take on that chestnut stud. Hellfire, if that kid'd been as good as they said, he'd've seen the kick coming and got out of the way. His own damned fault, that hole in his head. Just ask Buckminster; he'd tell you whose fault it was.

Only thing Martin Smith ever did right was shooting that damned stud colt where he stood. Might better have shot the wrangler along with the horse. Get both of them out'a their misery. Now that stupid son, he was laid out and rubbed daily by the ugly bitch called herself a woman, a widow. Mrs. Miller, goddamn her. Good reason for the poor son to wake up and not see much of nothing, having to find that old baggage handle him and stare at him while he was plumb helpless. Buckminster found he was almost in sympathy with a man he didn't even know. The mere thought of kindness turned his gut, and he wished for more of the warm, stale beer.

Damn fool Tom Miller ordered him a bride by mail and went and fell in love with the big cow. Buckminster hadn't believed what he'd seen till he put a hand on the woman and she banged him hard on the head with her fry pan. Knocked him clean to his knees instead of just saying no, thank you to his advances. He'd only wanted the feel of something warm and female, not like the ladies up to E-town. Not like those ladies who painted themselves up and wanted hard cash for a man to climb on them.

All he'd wanted was the touch of something warm and female in his hand, and the big cow'd banged him down to the floor. She felt that way 'bout old Tom Miller; she sure wouldn't take kindly to Buckminster's wishing to court her now. Word got out quick in a small town, and most knew the Cutheart'd failed. Spud Morgan already moved on, the payroll weeks late, dollars short. No one wanted Albert Buckminster with no cash in his pocket.

The bright sun hurt those tired eyes of his. Buckminster rubbed them and smelled old sweat and beer on his skin. Hell, he'd had to walk too many miles them days past when the team ran and got busted. Roan mare, she was ridable, but the lamed gelding brought only a few pennies down to the knackers. Hell on a man, not having a good horse. Or a good woman.

There was Frank Springer now, caught up with his brother and Martin Smith, grinning and talking and figuring how to make more money. Money could belong to Buckminster, but these sons, they wouldn't let old Buckminster have the backside of their profit.

He could learn to hate Frank Springer and his brother, alongside the man-size hatred he was growing for Martin Smith.

God, his mind was getting away fast with him; it was the thought of that big, old, ugly woman upstairs tending to the wrangler that got him going. Tried courting Smith's child this spring, when the Cutheart looked good. Slicked himself up real pretty, groomed out the gelding and the roan mare and even swept dirt out of the wagon. Bought up a boiled white shirt and hard collar, a new suit, got his hair cropped and slicked back and even cleaned his fingernails like the swells.

The beer soured on him again and he spit hard, thought about relieving himself right here in the street, but too many nosy folks would watch, and he didn't want to lose track of Smith and those Springers. So he rubbed his gut and pressed against the small of his back, and his mind got away from him again.

Turned out he had come to the Broken S the wrong time. Smith weren't there; he knew that, gambled on the man being up to Denver or Trinidad again, talking big deals, making up a fuss. But his timing was still bad.

That blond-headed cowboy come quick out of a small cabin, a Spencer dangling real easy from his right hand, eyes steadied in on Buckminster's shiny face. And the Indian, Peter Charley, he was called, he come out too, fancy rifle cradled across his chest. Both men not bothering to raise and sight their weapons, as if Albert Buckminster was more a nuisance than a real threat.

He could take him a hatred for that blond wrangler and the damned Indian for the insult. He'd filed that one, packed it in the back of his mind and let it fester and grow some, before he took it out for more study. Right now he saw the worst of them across the street, talking, figuring. The half-dead wrangler and the Indian, they could wait their turn in line.

First there was Martin Smith. And the big, ugly woman who knocked Albert Buckminster down with a fry pan.

Martin Smith could not help but see the misshapen bulk of the big man wobble and buck against the corner building across the street. At first, when he had come from the hotel interior, he was alarmed by Buckminster's vigil. Then he saw the man was only drunk and promptly forgot him.

Ranch business finally had him; lost in the nightmare of Elizabeth's illness and dying, he had let slip too many things that were necessary. Somewhere in the muddle of death, he had forgotten who he was. Martin Smith, rancher.

That fact never let go, and once again, today, he was faced with its reality. One Levi Preston had surveyed the land, eyed the water, and left his mark in a brief report. Frank Springer had caught up with Martin, reminded him of the importance of those few written words. Then Charles, too, spoke up about their importance.

Levi Preston proposed that a wall of only one hundred feet, a dam across the river, could provide enough water year-round to irrigate the fields and remove the ranchers from the whim of nature.

It wasn't Martin Smith and others like him who came to the Cimarron River land early who were so at the mercy of the elements. Smith had filed on good land, with good river-water rights. But the latecomers still felt the summer drought, the dry fall, the windswept winters that froze the cattle and blew away the melting snow. Water under man's control could change this yearly despair, as the Indians and the Spanish had done centuries past. Water running through ditches, from behind the hundred foot dam, could once again flood the land and raise fat cattle, good winter hay.

Levi Preston wrote his thoughts, left his mark, and moved on; Martin Smith was captured by the simple concept and awed by its possibilities. So once more he joined himself to the fortunes of the Springer brothers, who had proved so capable in their past glories.

He watched Charles Springer climb into his carriage. He was much like his brother in appearance but so different in his qualities. A rancher where Frank was a lawyer and newspaperman, a quiet man devoted to the land and cattle, building a dynasty from his new ranch house. Two men willing to share a good idea with those committed to hard work.

Smith waited on the steps, tired beyond his years. The scene in the dark sickroom played out again in his mind; too much like Elizabeth, too familiar in the smells and fever, yet a new study in futility because of the wounded man's youth and vigor, his growing strength, and his inevitable, complete blindness.

He let the sun bake into him, welcoming the summer warmth. He had been cold for days now, chilled through his hands and feet, an ache deep in his old bones. Old and yet the world did not slow down for him, wait for him. Here was another battle shaping up, a new force pitted against old ideas. Here was an idea that carried greatness and failure in it side by side. Power, greed, wealth, starvation, all lurked within the dam, and Martin Smith was stalled by the enormity of the project. For the first time he sensed the end of his life, the finish of his acts, the mortality of his flesh.

He stood a lonely man, lost in the bright sun of midday. His cold hands rubbed together for imagined warmth, his frail head bowed to the earth, his eyes closed in saddened fear.

His daughter would marry, and his wife's death would no longer matter. His own death was close. He stared up at the window of the hotel's second floor. An imagined shadow of a big woman moved across the shaded glass. His head dropped, his jowls shook, and even the touch of one hand on the other was painful, reminding him of his impending death. A new battle about to be fought and a commander who was dying.

"Martin, may I speak candidly with you?" Horace Farmer,

a familiar voice from years of futilely tending Elizabeth. Interrupting this time exactly when most needed. "Martin, we have a problem." More familiar words, common troubles and deeds that needed correcting. Anything that would divert Martin's thoughts from their endless rote of death. "Martin, are you ill?" The voice was in its practiced concern usually reserved for less well known patients. Martin Smith shook himself to regain control and raised his eyes in a more seemly gesture of command.

"I am fine, Horace, only disturbed by what occurred upstairs earlier. Perhaps Mrs. Miller has told you?" There, remove the worry from his own shaking bones and transfer it to the easier problem of the injured cowboy. Horace was quite simple to manipulate: drinking had dulled his mind to the more complex issues, so Martin believed.

"That is precisely why I have come looking for you. Young Mitchell is most definitely on the road to physical recovery. His fever is down, and he is now able to hold solid food. His strength will come back rapidly. I am always amazed at the recuperative powers of these young men. In my training . . ." Yes, Horace always managed to insert his eastern medical training into a conversation of any length. But as Horace went on, it was obvious that the miracle of Blue Mitchell's recovery was not all to the good.

"The young man is blind, Martin. Totally blind. He will not ever regain his sight. And there is nothing more I can do, except to prescribe a sedative when he becomes too much for Mrs. Miller's care. A nerve was damaged . . . there is nothing more to be done."

Horace Farmer rested his hand on his friend's arm and continued. "We cannot simply turn the young man out onto the street. There must be some way in which he can be cared for, some manner in which he may live with small comfort." Horace was a friend as well as a physician, but he was neither subtle nor very bright. He was directed by a good heart, which suffered at the sight of pain and was eased only by the temper of good whiskey.

What he was telling was not new to Martin Smith; the

unalterable facts rode with him each time he came into Cimarron and saw the square stone visage of the St. James Hotel. Blue Mitchell's life belonged to him now, Blue Mitchell's future was solely in Martin Smith's decision.

The simplest course was to bring Mitchell out to the Broken S and let him recover, when Horace felt it possible to move the young man. What happened next worried Martin Smith. A problem without a solution. Martin rubbed his hands together, they were unbearably cold. A vague idea came to him, but it was outrageous and unsettling.

Mitchell was young and strong, as Horace kept pointing out. The blindness did not drain his physical strength or wound his mind. He was a fine young man, and he was owed a great deal by Martin Smith.

The first step was to bring the patient back to the Broken S; beyond that Martin did not choose to go.

What was done with a healthy blind man?

Buckminster still watched, gloating when Smith stood alone, a prime target on the hotel steps. He imagined the bullet making its course, he felt the impact, saw the spurt of blood. And had the grace finally to laugh at himself. It would be a fool's work to shoot Martin Smith, but the fantasy was pleasing. Sweet revenge was better than hanging for a moment's death. He licked his lips as if tasting the already ripening fruit. The Cutheart mine was dead, the horses long ago sold for a pittance, the land consigned to others. The blame lay on Martin Smith's head. The man was already buried in Buckminster's mind. Whiskey would be the final toast, good whiskey as befitting the man's stature.

Buckminster yanked on his sagging pants and felt the few coins remaining in his pockets. It wasn't enough, and it didn't much matter.

Diaz's path was blocked. He did not jump and try to run, but waited patiently, already knowing what would be asked of him. The fat man thought Diaz was afraid, respectful of his size and power. It was not fear, it was the need for a few coins that kept Diaz waiting.

"The best bottle, kid, only the best for Albert Buckminster." The coins held in the gritty hand were pitiful, but it was clear currency for Diaz, since it was Señor Lambert's whiskey he was selling.

The storeroom with the good whiskey was locked and left unwatched. Diaz had paid attention and knew the whereabouts of the key. And he knew how to cut the whiskey that was opened and fool even the fancy Frenchman's taste. It might be stealing to those fortunate to have a little of their own; to Diaz and his tribe, it was a clever way to earn small wealth.

Diaz was a foundling, a mixed breed among hundreds who existed on the edge of the more proper world. He was ignorant of many things, but he was not stupid. He would not steal too much from a man like Señor Lambert, who fed him and allowed him to work. There had been others who cared, who taught him the basics, how to read a few letters, to sign his name at the bottom of the page. He could add sums, and he could remember directions. Then there were those who would teach him more, wanting for their pleasure his smooth skin and his youth. These he escaped, as he fled the institution where his mama had placed him.

There was nothing wrong in his world with taking a bottle or two and making a few pennies. He retraced his steps and found Buckminster leaning on the wall; the fat man's face was red, and sweat dripped down the dirty cheeks, tracing a messy path. Diaz wondered if the man was sick and then found he did not care when the coin was dropped in his hand and the bottle was exchanged. There was no need for contact with this ugly brute, Diaz would finish his simple chores in the kitchen and then go back upstairs, to see if Señora Miller had need of him.

It was not necessary for him to go upstairs. She had not called, and it was not his usual time. But if he appeared at the doorway and the strange young man was quiet or asleep, and Señora Miller was soft and her eyes were moist, she

89

would talk to Diaz. She would tell him strange stories and make him laugh, and then she would wipe his hair from his eyes and stroke his face, and the touch of her hand pleased him more than anything he could remember.

He rode a wild mare, a thing untamed. He clung to her ribs and backbone and held her with his knees, his hands woven in her dark mane. He rode her like he had not ridden before, head thrown back, mouth open to drink in the air. Eyes shut tight; he rode blind and screamed in the freedom. The mare raced, ears flat, and he was screaming for her to run.

The words stopped him, and he fought them, grabbed for them, and caught live flesh between his hands. He came awake heavily, with his hands on soft flesh, his arms rigid, his eyes still unseeing. It was the screams and the hated words that awakened him. He came back to the airless room and the wet sheets, the damp pillows that smothered him.

Words hit at him, scourging across his face. "Please let go, please, you're hurting me. Señor . . ." The voice rose to a childish wail, and Blue recognized the pleading sounds. The child who came in daily to remove the stinking chamber pot.

The smell each time shamed Blue, as if he could change the functions of his body by the efforts of his mind. He was a fool.

"My God, boy. I'm sorry. I didn't mean . . . ahhh." As if he didn't know the right words to apologize. He had not meant to hurt the boy, who was only doing his job.

"It is no matter, señor. I did not think you were awake. I came in only to help the señora. I am the one who is to apologize."

"I ain't good at this, boy. What's your name? I'm the one done wrong, I'm the one needs to say sorry." Blue heard his own voice, and hated what he had done. Gone after a boy doing his job. "Look, forget it. Next time you best knock. I can't see you, boy."

The child interrupted him softly, saying, "My name is Diaz, señor."

The few words gave Blue time to catch the self-pity in his own words. "I can't see much of nothing, Diaz. So you best knock even if I'm sleeping peaceful. Best for both of us."

The smell ripened quickly in the cramped room. Blue wrinkled up his face. "Ah, yes, we must do something about this mess. I must do something. . . ." The boy was clever, older than Blue had first thought. Much wiser than Blue had ever been. To willingly accept responsibility and make Blue feel inferior at the same time. A real clever one, Diaz.

He sorted through the noises, knew Diaz was removing what he could of Blue's destructive awakening. The enamel pan rang out once, and Blue cringed from the shame. To have another person clean up after him; he could not get used to this.

His eyes hurt, and he rubbed them unthinkingly, against the doc's direct orders. He winced, yet there was short relief. His head ached now, especially where the horse had kicked him.

He remembered it all and sat up, opened his mouth. He heard a muffled shout and thought of the poor kid called Diaz. It weren't the kid's fault, not this time, not the first time either.

"Diaz, you're a smart one, so tell me. It was the big chestnut colt what got me, right? The one Smith owns. Ahh . . . I heard a shot, tried to move, but my head hurt. Something fell. There was blood, I smelled it. Lots of blood. I tried to ask, but no one could hear me. Diaz, tell me. That chestnut colt, he kicked me? What the hell happened?"

It took effort to hold his temper, and his gut revolted on him, soured into his mouth. Now he knew, now he touched the sore place on his head and felt the bone give way. He'd been kicked, bad. He was blind. He had to accept that—he was blind.

Something must have showed on his face, something he wanted to hide; a hand smoothed the sheet around his legs, and a voice told him to lie back, be quiet, it would be all right.

The woman'd come into the room; he knew that much

91

right off. He wondered if the kid, Diaz, had called her. She was crying now; he could hear the change in her voice, the sob buried in her throat. "Ma'am, my eyes itch, that's all. I'm restless, kind'a wanting to get going. You know, I been here too long. Caused that kid all kinds of grief. Just restless, that's all."

Then because he hated himself and hated the boy and the tall woman because they were watching him, seeing his weakness, he lied to them with a smile forced on his face, and the lie hurt him deeper than he would have thought. "Ma'am, you take these bandages off my eyes, I'll be fine. Let me see, and I won't cause you no more trouble."

His hands betrayed him as they rubbed the thin skin of his eyelids, and the betrayal made his words more terrible.

"Ma'am, you take off these damned bandages and let me see, and I'll be fine. You'll see. Just get these damned things off my eyes."

TEN

POOR CHILD, TO think it was only cloth that kept him from seeing. How tragic, to be young and suddenly helpless. Lela Miller inhaled deeply and knew what must have happened. The evidence was on the floor, staining the bedclothes, and ripening in the air.

She set the boy, Diaz, to cleaning up the mess, while she tried to comfort poor Mr. Mitchell. When she perched tentatively on the edge of the bed and gently touched Mr. Mitchell's arm, he flinched from her, pulled back into the depth of the feather mattress.

Much earlier than this, Lela Miller had convinced herself that such a reaction was not due to her looks but to the man's inherent fear. He could not see; therefore, he could not see what touched him unexpectedly. She should have spoken first. All he knew from the disaster was her harsh speech to Diaz and the sounds of the cleanup effort.

"It is only me, Mr. Mitchell. Your nurse. It is all right now, I will help you. Just lie still, lie back and rest. I will take care of you."

It meant so much to be caring for this young man. He needed her. That could be seen by his head lolling on his chest, his refusal to lie down until she used her hand to force him, for his own good. Still the strange eyes remained open, and their vacant stare wandered across the room. When they stopped near where Diaz was finishing the chore, she wondered briefly, for only a moment, if the young man perhaps could see.

Then the eyes rolled back in his head, and he collapsed more than lay back in the bed, and Lela Miller knew she was right. He needed her like no one, except for Thomas Miller, had ever needed her. She was not willing to give up the odd and wonderful sensation so soon after Thomas's premature death.

It was then that Lela Miller saw the wide stain on the floor and a similar one on the bedclothes of her patient. He must have felt her concern, for he sat up quickly, swaying as he put his bare feet over the bedside and planted them on the sticky floor.

"Ma'am. I apologize . . . ain't been this way since I was a pup. I . . ." He sagged as if suddenly come to the end of his strength. She put out her hands, and tucked one under each arm to gently support his torso. The face so close to her whitened, and the mouth thinned, lost all color. Then, as quickly, the mouth moved in a small, rare smile, and Lela Miller's heart fluttered. The odd eyes half opened and once again moved as if they could see. She was struck by their terrible lost beauty.

She let him lean against her bosom. "This is no disgrace, Mr. Mitchell. You have been sick, you are still sick. Please, don't worry."

As he allowed her to lay him down in the bed, she knew from the lax feel of his arms that her Blue Mitchell was safe for a few more days, even weeks. He would not be getting up alone quite yet. He was still dependent upon Lela Miller, still her patient, at the mercy of her competent, willing hands and lonely woman's heart.

The wind took Flora's breath away. She automatically swept her hair from her eyes and raised her right hand once again to whip the shoulder of the dark bay gelding she rode. The horse leapt from the blow, and the wind tormented Flora's eyes until she shut them and gave herself completely to the wild running.

94

Like her father, she thought. Like he gloried in his horses, so she basked in their speed and power. She rode astride and wore the same pants she had worn for her lesson with the horse trainer when her father was not at the ranch.

She disdained the conventions, when her father was not at the ranch. She was free, for this short moment; she was wild and untouchable, let loose in her own world. Her mouth strained to swallow, and her lungs screamed for more air as the bay gelding flattened down and raced the long dirt road. This was her freedom, her eyes glazed with the effort to see, her hands stuck to the coarse, sweat-soaked reins, and she clamped her legs to the hard saddle. The body of a fallen cottonwood blocked her path, she guided the slowing bay towards it, struck the unwilling horse again, and experienced the all-too-brief joy of flying.

Then she was aware of the thudding heart of the tired bay and heard the sound of labored breathing. She was not consciously cruel, and in the moment of becoming aware of the horse, she thought of Blue Mitchell and slowed the bay to a walk. The horse shook his head, the heavy mane flopping. The salt smell of thick sweat rose and tantalized Flora. The air was soft. A bird chirped in the grass across the river. Late shadows told her the time, and that her father could be in the house wandering the empty rooms, calling her name and wishing for his wife.

Buckminster grabbed the handle of the heavy door and tugged. He was almost sober; it was the end of the day. The bank was a small, unimposing structure built of adobe brick and wood. The glass in the front doors was milky, to afford privacy for the internal transactions. Buckminster hesitated, pretending he was not nervous. He thought that Lucien Maxwell himself could have built the building, Maxwell being a most practical man. Finally Buckminster opened the door.

Once he was inside, it made no difference about the origins of the building or its designer. The banker himself, Hadden Hooper, came out from behind his narrow desk to tell Buckminster in brief words that there was no hope of a loan. Word was out on the Cutheart and other mines. And there were no loans to be had.

Of course Hooper was mighty sorry, so he proclaimed, that he couldn't help; he even put a short, plump arm around Buckminster's shoulder in condolence, but the gesture was awkward and forced, and both men quickly dropped the pretense of civility. As quickly as he had received the news, Buckminster was back on the steps, the door closed firmly behind him. Broke, and no prospects.

The late sun hit him square on. He blinked and licked his dry lips, tasting the remains of good whiskey. A swallow of that good stuff would set well right now. Hold his temper down, give him room to figure. There was a bottle back in his room, up over the general store. Smooth, free-running whiskey that could light up a soul with pure pleasure. Not many men in this damned town could drink the good stuff and know the difference. Not many men were as educated as Albert Buckminster.

The coin he'd got off the miserable hide and tallow of that lamed gelding what run off with him was almost gone. So the bottle up in his room was likely the last of the good stuff for a long while. Buckminster began a careful trip across town, angling toward the false front of the cavernous general store. He didn't want to think on the fact that he was busted, broke, flat turned out and down for a loan. Left with a no-good roan mare eating up hay and doing nothing, and a dried-out saddle, rotted saddle bags, a good knife, and a rusting pistol.

A habit born out of years of physical danger stopped Buckminster at the base of the narrow stairs that rose to his hot room. He looked right and left, watched the pattern of the horse traffic, took note of who was walking within his range.

He saw plump, foolish Hadden Hooper poke his head out of that milk-glass double door and call out something, then push open the door and trot down the street looking for all the world like a tamed sheep bleating for its master.

Sure enough, there was Martin Smith headed toward Longacre's Livery. The old man stopped and turned. He met up with Hooper, and they stood close, Hooper talking and waving his arms wildly. Buckminster knew, without hearing any words, what was talked over; he knew with a cold, clear sense that his loan had been refused at Martin Smith's request, and now Hooper was carrying the glad news.

If they thought Buckminster could be easily pushed out, they sure as hell didn't know their opponent. The two separated. Hooper trotted back down the walk, coattails flopping, white hair fussing in the wind. It was Smith himself who checked the street, out of old habit, and those cold blue eyes caught hold of Buckminster and raked him over, even with the distance far between them.

Buckminster ached for a pistol in hand. No one could hear his tale and deny him his right to kill, but he was naked, stripped by convention, his pistol and remaining shells hanging from a nail in the room waiting above him.

All that was left was ponderous dignity. Buckminster drew himself up proudly, stiffened, and walked heavily up the wobbly stairs. He might be the obvious loser now, to those who had watched the silent exchange. But he would not remain the loser for long. Solace awaited him in the belly of the whiskey bottle and the well-worn grips of his pistol and the old rifle, which had stood him well. He was not yet defeated, he was regrouping, planning, readying to launch a powerful attack. But first he needed a drink of whiskey.

Hooper's tirade drained Martin Smith's fading energy. It was a list of new failures. Two more mines closed down, a rancher south of town, near Rayado, had lost more than half his spring calves to a poison weed. Now Jenkins up to the mouth of Ponil Canyon said elk were destroying his summer range, and Buttram's usual winter grass had been nipped clean by a newcomer's strayed flock of sheep.

He needed to get home. It was late, almost dusk, and Flora would be alone, fretting in the abandoned house. He climbed on the chestnut mare and even let old Longacre hold her bridle while he did so. It was an admission of his age, and worse still he did not care. Not when he was so tired that his arms ached when he lifted them to the saddle, not when his knees shook once he climbed aboard the obedient mare. He was old, losing all the things once important to him. There were no more replacements, only empty holes where his joy had once been.

Smith let the mare step into a rocking lope, then had to draw her back to a sedate walk. His soul needed the running, his lungs needed the cool air. He would laugh at himself for his aging, but he could not find enough air to cough up a sound. He let the mare walk and paid no attention when she stopped several times to graze along the lush river grass. It was dark when he reined the mare toward the shadow of the barn and the patient Peter Charley. It had begun to feel like he would never get home.

Flora was just inside the door; he could see her outline from the lamp set on the table. He started toward his child, hesitated, and turned back. "Peter Charley, I know you and Mitchell, well, you kind of are alike. He's better now, much better. Doc says he'll be fine. The rest . . . we don't know. If . . . you might take it in mind to go see him. He'd . . . well, in any case."

The night had turned cold, not uncommon even in midsummer. Flora had a fire burning. The smell tantalized him, the feel of the warmth eased him as he stood in front of the flame and rubbed his hands together. They would not thaw out, no matter how hard he rubbed them.

He stopped abruptly. His child wore pants; his daughter was dressed like a man. Her body was clearly detailed for any man's eye. The white shirt she wore was dirty, stained with green on the shoulder, and unbuttoned at the collar, so that the swell of her bosom was most noticeable. The reddish hair, so much like her mother's, was tied back and tangled. Strands curved along her neck and touched her mouth. Her skin was flawless; she was utterly beautiful.

He was shocked and opened his mouth to reprimand his child. But he found he had no words, no speech at all. She behaved as if nothing was wrong, nothing out of place. She came toward him with a crystal glass containing a fine amber

98

liquid. As she handed the glass to him, she smiled shyly and tilted her head, and the gesture was so much Elizabeth that Martin Smith wanted to cry.

ELEVEN

IT WAS GOING to be hot today, even for midsummer. Mrs. Miller carried the tray lightly, a renewed spring in her steps as she marched up the front stairs. The tray held a cooked egg, two tortillas, and a few beans. More than Mr. Mitchell had eaten in a long time. But after yesterday, and the previous days, after his weakening and raising such a fuss, she determined with a consultation with Dr. Farmer that their patient could begin to try solid foods. He needed his strength, although Mrs. Miller did not think, as the doctor seemed to, that the young man was ready to begin walking. He still needed to rest in bed, still needed her constant care.

He was sitting up when she came to the open door. She could see the pale white of a foot sticking out beneath the covers, and before she entered, his head turned toward her and his voice cried out, a note of panic quite evident. "Who's there, what do you want? . . . Who is it?"

She was quick to reassure him and was pleased at the look on his face. Of course he still needed her; he could not see. Didn't the good doctor remember that, or had he been drinking too much again? Blue Mitchell could not see, and he needed her for the simplest thing.

But he refused to let her feed him, and that was disquieting. She sat on the bed in her usual place and held the tray out for him. It was fascinating to watch those deft hands seek out the food, and she almost laughed with him when he stuck a finger directly into the yolk of the egg. There—now he would ask for her help. But he touched on the tortillas and folded one to use as a scoop. She did raise the plate to his mouth, to catch the drip of egg as it slid from the bread, but she had to admit she had never fully appreciated the use of the tortilla until she watched Blue eat his ruined egg. There was yolk staining his mouth, but he had gotten most of the food without knife or fork.

Then he grinned at her, and the uneasy feeling of not being needed disappeared. He looked so odd; bits of egg at the corners of his mouth, white flecks of the bread in his straggly beard, a strand of dirty hair over one eye. He looked much like a waif, a street urchin finishing his first good meal.

His face suddenly turned gray, and he shuddered, rattling the plate and cup on the tray. Mrs. Miller stood up quickly and swept the tray from his lap. He lay back on the bed without her having to prompt him, and one thin hand came up in great effort to wipe at the tired mouth. A yellow stain was smeared across the pale skin.

The blind eyes opened then, their startling color disturbing her. Once again Mrs. Miller leaned over her beloved patient, and, using the tips of two fingers, she drew the eyelids back over their sightless orbs. She was startled and then deeply wounded when she identified tears coming from under the closed lids. As if her ministrations were not sufficient, as if her care was less than perfection.

She could not desert him, she could not go out into the hall and cry for herself—not yet. Not while he needed her. She was careful to put the tray and its mangled contents on the small table away from the bed, and she used the napkin, moistened in a pitcher of water she kept nearby, to wipe away the stubborn egg yolk. The linen napkin was of fine quality; Monsieur Lambert had only the best for his hotel.

It was not Blue Mitchell's fault that he was injured, it was not his fault that she had come to love him. He was at her mercy, despite Dr. Farmer's enthusiasm, and she must rise above petty insults and continue with her Christian duty. He had eaten two bites of his breakfast by himself before collapsing. He needed her today as much as he had yesterday and all the preceding days. She would be waiting for him tomorrow.

Mrs. Miller was able to feed her patient two more bites of the egg and a torn corner of the tortilla. He even drank some of the goat's milk sent over especially for him. Then he rolled his head helplessly and shut his mouth and would not eat more. That was enough, she thought. It would not do to get him upset or distressed. He was, after all, bedridden and must not be assaulted too quickly by the demands of the outside world.

Couldn't Dr. Farmer understand, that to get up and walk, and bump into walls, would be terrible? That to sit by a window where he could feel the fresh air and hear the voices, but not see any of the activity, would destroy his confidence and slow his recovery?

She had only the best intentions for her patient, and only her endless, loving care would assist the young man in accepting his new lot in the world, which had once dazzled him into reckless abandon. He needed time, and the love of his nurse, to help him acquiesce to his blind handicap.

Couldn't the good doctor understand?

His head ached and his mouth was dry. Buckminster rolled over and spit on the floor, then rolled back and covered his throbbing eyes. The last of the bottle had tasted good, taking away the bitter shame of his present condition, letting him laugh for the moment.

Now he wanted a new bottle of whiskey, good whiskey, and a quart of coffee and someone to empty the stinking pot under his bed. He must have been sick in the night; he didn't remember, but his head ached and his mouth tasted bad, his throat was raw and the room smelled worse than usual.

The big man struggled to sit up on the edge of the rumpled bed. He still had his boots on, and his spurs. As if he had a decent horse to ride. The thin blanket covering the mattress was torn, and the stuffing showed. The old lady who rented out the room wouldn't be too pleased. He'd had the edge of her tongue before, and he ducked his head at the mere thought.

Hell, Buckminster thought. He didn't have to care what the old baggage thought. He stood up and dug through his pants pockets. A quarter, minted new and shiny, was his remaining wealth. Not enough, so he'd have to scare the kid to the St. James into getting a bottle. A quarter and a threat would earn Buckminster his last whiskey.

His thick hands shook while he tried to button his pants. He couldn't catch up with the narrow buttons and soon gave up, cursing the manufacturer of the pants and the world in general while he was getting started. After a taste from the bottle, he'd be fine. He'd button his pants and stare the whole goddamn place right in the eye. Spit, too, if anyone crossed him.

He could almost grin as he walked out into the sunshine. He regretted not wearing a hat, but it was a short walk down street and cross-lot to the steps of the St. James. After his bottle, he'd get his hat and shade his eyes. Hell, he'd feel so good he might get himself a bath and a shave, maybe his hair trimmed. He felt the ragged edges of his hair, and the strands slipped through his greasy fingers. He opened his eyes wider against the bright sun and saw again the single quarter in his hand. A lot to do, after he had his good whiskey.

Diaz saw the fat man and knew there was trouble. He knew about the refused loan; everyone knew about the death of the Cutheart. That was old news. Trouble walked across the street, shambling like a winter-starved bear, big hands loose at the thick sides, head bare, the bald spot exposed and silly.

It was almost funny to watch the fat man; he stumbled when the Laytons' pug dog nipped at his heels, and came close to falling when he tried to kick and got tangled in his own feet. A walking sideshow—when he stopped near the corner, maybe to judge the long distance from there to the St. James, the fat man put out a hand to lean on a tree and missed. Diaz laughed out loud and quickly put a hand over his mouth, as if the fat devil could hear him.

He could disappear inside the belly of the hotel; no one knew the St. James as well as Diaz, not even the sainted, hot-tempered Henri Lambert. But there was a slyness in the fat man, with a temper to match. Diaz believed the man would hunt him down no matter the cost, to have his whiskey at Diaz's expense.

So he was not sure when Buckminster loomed in front of him with only one shiny quarter to have his bottle. Diaz shook his head while beginning to try and explain it was not enough, and Buckminster picked him up with one hand around his neck. Diaz heard the tearing of cloth and knew his skin could be torn also. He choked and coughed, but Buckminster had no pity.

Still, he could not risk stealing Lambert's fine whiskey for so small a profit.

Diaz hung in the air, his feet kicking above solid ground. Buckminster's face was too close, his breath a cesspool. The whole man stank of sweat and vomit. Diaz was not fussy, but he had standards, and the fat man crossed the line. He could see into the face, and it was bright red. The eyes were glazed, and the smell was unbearable. Then Buckminster roared and bared his teeth, and Diaz knew how a kitten in the mouth of a tiger felt.

He was shaken by the fat man, his head snapped back, and his arms and legs dangled. Diaz raised one knee and caught Buckminster squarely in the crotch.

The big hands opened, and Diaz fell. The hands went to the source of pain and clutched bruised flesh. Buckminster groaned loudly, and the foul air choked Diaz as he struggled to stand. The fat man knelt before Diaz, both hands cupped to his genitals; the red eyes were squeezed shut, the foul mouth sagged open, and terrible noises came from the wounded monster.

Diaz scrambled backward, in awe of the terrible sounds. The fat man began to cry, and Diaz was terrified. He had not meant such great harm; he had only meant to escape his immediate death. Sweat poured from the fat man, the huge body shook violently, and Diaz, on hands and knees, watched in open-mouthed terror.

He did not hear the footsteps. He did not know the presence of another man until the accented voice spoke with a soft query as to the problem. The words were in English in deference to Diaz's lack of knowledge in French.

"Perhaps the man is sick?" asked Henri Lambert, the owner of the St. James, the proprietor, as he was called. Diaz wanted to run, but he was still on hands and knees and completely humiliated. His chest hurt as if his heart was punching a hole through it, and his ribs thudded with fear. He began to shake, much as the fat man still shook, and Diaz could not find the muscles that opened and shut his mouth and produced recognizable sounds.

The hotel owner seemed to understand; he placed a hand on Diaz's shoulder and offered the boy a moment's grace. "We must remove this man from our hotel. He is not welcome as our guest in such a state. I will not have him hurt you or anyone who works for me, is loyal to me." Diaz's heart shattered. He had not paid Lambert well for his trust. "Diaz, stand up, child. Go get us some help, two big men, and we will remove this offal from our sight. Hurry."

It was a relief to move. Diaz giggled; they would need two oxen or a team of mules to drag that much fat out of the way. But he found Benito and Carl, and they did as their boss directed. They literally dragged Albert Buckminster from the dark tunnel to the kitchen and left the man outside in the sun, away from any connection to the St. James and its reputation.

Diaz expected to be fired or yelled at, even hit. But Lambert, he did no such thing; he only asked Diaz quietly what had happened, how he had so effectively maimed the fat man. Diaz told a halting tale, using his broken English as a way to not tell the whole story. He would no longer steal from Henri Lambert, but he was not willing to make a confession, not yet.

Lambert listened and only shook his head. He left orders that the big man, Albert Buckminster, was not to be allowed back inside the St. James. Before he went back to other duties, Lambert stared hard at Diaz and asked the question again without speaking the words. But Diaz was not ready and acted as if he did not understand. So Lambert frowned and told Diaz the truth. "I do not yet know if you will stay. I am not certain of all you have told me. Be careful, young Diaz, that big man will not forget what you have done. Nor will I."

Ten minutes later, Diaz found the courage to look outside the back door, and there was no sign of the fat man. He went to the front, into the formal parlor, where he was not allowed to be. But fear overrode his concern for the rules, and he pulled back the edge of a long lace curtain and checked up and down the street. He could see only Martin Smith, at the livery, with one of his fine horses, talking to the funny old man who owned the stable and could be mean if teased. Buckminster was nowhere in sight.

But Diaz knew, now that he was no longer frightened, that the story about the fat man's being thrown out of the St. James, and Diaz's part in the tale, would go quickly around the small town. He was terrified all over again and began to giggle; Buckminster would hear the story and he would come looking for Diaz. He would wait on the other side of the St. James's safety and pick up Diaz in those huge hands. This time he would kill Diaz before anyone could stop him. Diaz giggled fitfully. Laughter would kill him as quickly as a bolt of lightning or a crazed horse.

Diaz was truly in trouble. It was time for him to leave the small town and the life he had made in it. But he did not yet wish to leave. There were good people here, good food, a dry, comfortable place for him to sleep. And he would miss the clumsy woman upstairs who scolded him and then patted his arm and pushed his dark hair out of his eyes.

And then, too, there was the blinded horse tamer who sat up in bed and made jokes with Diaz.

He did not want to leave Cimarron, not yet.

Diaz was not the only one to see Martin Smith again in conversation with old Longacre. Albert Buckminster sat on the edge of a three-legged stool in his hot room and stared out through the filthy window, intent on the activity below, imagining it revolved around him. His gut still ached, and his testicles were swollen enough that it was difficult to walk, or urinate, without pain. He held a new grudge, against the skinny breed who enticed him into the St. James with the promise of good whiskey and then brought Albert Buckminster to his knees.

Being brought down by a skinny kid was the height of humiliation for Buckminster. He was in disgrace, and while he sat, he planned out more revenge.

His quarter and a fist rammed into the man's face had bought a pint of bar booze from Joe Morris of the Silver Eye. It pained Buckminster to take the first drink, and he almost spit out the brutal liquor. Then it burned and settled in his belly, and he began to feel better. He had finished more than half of the bottle in less than ten minutes and could barely stay on the stool and look out the window.

The new ache in his groin matched his pounding head, and he was flat busted. Buckminster scratched his head and felt the slicked hair; he stared out through the filth and saw Martin Smith and old Longacre. The runty stableman waved his hands wildly, and Buckminster thought he could hear Smith's laugh.

He hated both men fiercely. Then a third man joined the group, and Buckminster's ragged temper unraveled. Henri Lambert, that damned Frenchman, was with Smith and Longacre, and Longacre said something that had all of them laughing. Lambert got started then, and Buckminster could imagine the words chosen most carefully as the damned foreigner told of the morning's activities, the expulsion of Buckminster from his precious hotel. That breed kid would take a share of the glory, even if the blow he delivered had been a mistake.

It was too much, more than any decent man could be expected to take. The humiliation was bad enough, and then these three would make it public with their loud mouths and self-importance. Now that the big man was down on his luck, the town vulture, would gather 'round and take turns pecking at him, destroying flesh, shredding dignity.

The hatred that burned in Buckminster was refueled by the last of the rotgut whiskey. He stood up, towering over the tipsy stool, and threw the bottle against the far wall in his impotence. He howled until a pain deep in his vitals twisted, and he cried from its merciless void. The whiskey burned a hole, the humiliation flooded his brain. He went toward the bed, and his foot slipped. He cried out as he fell, reaching for the bed. His head cracked on the iron frame, and he was unconscious before hitting the floor. Dust rose in clouds from the impact, a cockroach moved off course by his bulk. A curious mouse appeared from under a door and watched for a moment until it decided the fallen man posed no great threat.

Across the dry, hot street, Martin Smith allowed Zach Longacre to take in the chestnut mare. He went with his friend, Henri Lambert, back into the coolness of the St. James Hotel, to sip at good brandy and talk of inconsequential matters.

TWELVE

Dᴇꜱᴘɪᴛᴇ ᴛʜᴇ ʙʟɪɴᴅɴᴇꜱꜱ, he could at least sit up. And if he was careful, he could find the pitcher of water and drink when he wanted to, not just when the woman offered it. He'd managed that much earlier in the day, what he guessed was day by the meal he tried to eat and the sounds from outside the window.

Now he was thirsty again and naturally had to relieve himself. Blue sat on the edge of the bed, his bare feet firmly planted wide apart on the floor. He listened intently, for once almost wishing the woman, or the kid, would appear at the door. He wasn't good at asking for anything, but he could not ignore his basic needs.

Hell, he was thirsty. And hot. He reached out toward the right, felt the height of the glass pitcher, and then knocked what must be the glass off the table. He heard it shatter and swore again. But the handle of the pitcher fitted in his hand and he could find his own mouth, so he drank from the heavy glass and used both hands to return it carefully to the table.

He rubbed his eyes reflectively; his head still ached and the eyes were dry and itchy. He didn't want to cut his damned feet, but he needed to get up.

He didn't even know where the chamber pot was, or maybe the kid had taken it downstairs and not returned it. He couldn't remember, been sleeping too much, tired all the time, half-groggy and fool-headed. He pressed the tips of his fingers against the sore spot at his temple and blinked hard from the pressure. Where that damned horse clipped him, healed but tender. Another damned reminder of his wasted life.

He still had to use the backhouse. He stood carefully, felt the cutting edge of glass under a big toe, and shoved it carefully out of reach. It wasn't a good beginning to his first steps on his own. So he took time, swept his right foot in an arc, and heard glass tinkle against more glass. He almost fell back on the bed. Lost his balance, too, he decided, along with his sight.

God, he hated the word "blind." Might as well shoot him as leave him this helpless. He wiped the floor clean with the left foot and came close again to sitting down on the bed. A bit of the glass stuck on his heel and he rubbed it off cautiously.

The first real steps were uneven and ragged, as if he were crippled. Then he got brave and took a big step and came down on broken glass. The small cut was no worse than the pressure at the small of his back and the need for relief. He cursed and hopped into the wall, hit his nose and cursed again. But he could lean forward with his rump on the wall, find his own foot, and pick out the glass. He threw it hard, and the sound it made hitting something tinny pleased him; he was getting sour in his old age.

There had to be a door, a way out of the room. Common sense could help him figure out where. He held still, breathed in, listened and tried to puzzle out the sounds. Muffled voices came from the left, got louder, and disappeared. Fresh air ruffled his hair on the right side of his face. So the window was to his right. He hopped toward the voices, favoring his cut foot, praying he was dead on in his guessing.

Hands waving in front of him, touching nothing, Blue stepped boldly and felt the ridge of a door frame. He was through the door; by God, he was out of the damned hole they'd called a room. Walking on his own! Wobbly, and free!

He grinned in spite of his weakness and wiped his face,

let go of the door and set out as if he knew where he was going. Three steps and the crooked floor groaned under his weight; four more steps and he could touch nothing with either hand.

Betraying sweat stung his eyes, and he rubbed hard, setting his head to its too familiar throbbing. Damn, he thought. Goddamn. I only want the backhouse. That ain't asking for much.

An odd noise alerted him before the voice came. He flinched anyway when the words were too close. First time a body got within reach of him without his knowing. Being blind weren't fun.

He inhaled, listened, knew it was the kid. Diaz. "Señor, you are not to be here. Señora Miller, she will be very angry."

The kid's voice had an odd ring to it. "You all right, boy? Sound kinda like you been wrestling a bear, or seen a wolf."

"Señor, you are half-naked. Señor Lambert, he will not like it if the guests see you like this."

So the kid wanted to hide his trouble; Blue understood that impulse. But no one was forcing him back into the small room and that damned bedpan again. "Diaz, you seen a buck-naked man before. And hell, you know where I'm headed. Steer me in the right direction, and Lambert's precious guests won't have to see a ghost."

"Señor?" The voice rose as if the kid did not understand. Blue was getting impatient and anxious. "Diaz, I ain't standing here to talk. You point me north or wherever the backhouse is, and stop bothering me with nonsense."

It was quite a picture to find in the elegance of the St. James. Diaz would have been amused except for his earlier scare. To meet up with the determination of a man such as Blue Mitchell, he was caught without thought or words. As if all sense had been scared out of him by the fat one, Buckminster.

But he could not help but smile at the sight before him; the long legs, bony feet, the nightshirt half hanging off the

111

thin body. The hair wild, the open eyes staring as if they could see. And a half smile on the face, as if Señor Mitchell could see himself and know the joke.

Then he saw a weakness come over the man, as if flooded by an outside force. The body shook, and the face turned pale and shiny from new sweat. Diaz acted quickly; he put out his arm, held the man's shoulders, felt the weight sag against him. But when he tried to turn Mitchell back, aim him toward the safety of the room, he found the true core of the man. "Diaz, I been in there too damn long. Now you help me to that damned backhouse and keep your thinking to yourself. I just need to piss, goddamnit!"

Whatever he said, it got the kid moving, and Blue couldn't find enough breath to thank him. His chest thudded, his ears rang, and his knees threatened mutiny with each step. But, by God, they was on their way down the hall and through a door where the smell came hot and strong, and Blue sighed. No stairs, though, and he thought to ask Diaz. The kid answered before he got the words going. "Yes, señor, it is on the second story. Only for the use of the guests if they must, in the middle of the night. I have seen nothing like it, and would not choose to be downstairs at a time such as this. Here you are, señor. I will leave you in peace."

A good kid, even though he weren't willing to talk up to a question. But Blue really didn't care. He could take care of himself now.

He started back, feeling the smooth carpet under his bare feet, running a hand along the wall for direction, trying to count doors and remember. But his head whirled and his lungs burned, and the empty space in front of his eyes showed white holes and drifting circles. He was getting dizzy and angry.

A new presence coughed to alert him, and Blue silently thanked the gesture. He wasn't good at this being helpless; he didn't like that anyone could sneak up on him.

It was a familiar voice, and he welcomed its sound. Martin Smith, standing somewhere ahead of Blue. "May I help, Mr.

Mitchell? You are a sight, a right cheerful sight. It is good to see you up and moving about."

So it was a relief for Smith to have Blue moving. Right then Blue would have gratefully sat down on the nearest anything could hold his weight. He was goddamn tired.

A hand cupped his elbow, and a shoulder touched his, giving support. He could smell brandy, cigars, and horses. "Thank you, Smith. I . . . godawful tired."

Uncombed and wild, stinking of hot flesh and exhaustion, Mitchell still had an air that Martin Smith admired. The young man muttered as he half rested on Martin, and the only intelligible word was "horses," spoken as a curse. Martin wondered if Mitchell were damning him, guessing at his lapse in the incident with the stallion.

It occurred to him to ask Mitchell, but the woman waited at the door of the sick room, and the look on her blanched face was enough to encourage all men to move to her bidding. She came forward, mouth pursed, eyes flaring an unmentioned anger. As if Martin Smith were to blame for all of it, everything. Especially the limp man now hanging from his arms in complete surrender.

He gave his burden over to Mrs. Miller and did not stay to watch her fold him onto the bed and pin him down with the tucked sheets and blankets. He had had enough. Martin Smith walked deliberately and quickly down the hotel stairs and through the lobby. He gave the appearance of a man who knew where he was going.

Outside, able to once again breathe and see, he shuddered. Furious at himself for a weakness once again revealed. He owed Blue Mitchell something, a debt not yet paid.

Other debts waited, other items not yet fully accounted. He was not making sense, he was wandering, a victim of age and a restless, unsettled mind.

Albert Buckminster haunted him; there was badness brewing, delayed, hidden. Waiting.

His child came to him last evening, laughing, listening, offering him a glass of good whiskey. And wearing man's pants, a revealing shirt tucked around her narrow waist. He had not seen such determination before. She was so much like her mother. He had missed a great many things about his child.

Blue Mitchell's face crowded his thoughts; he owed the man an enormous debt. He admired the undimmed spirit, and he wanted his youth, the tough muscle and beating heart, the lack of fear, the inevitable freedom. He wanted the youth, he coveted the years. He would trade places with Mitchell even in his blindness for the energy and toughness, the time still waiting.

Martin Smith drew himself up straight and placed a hand on the iron railing of the St. James Hotel, not for its support but for the heat of the metal, the remains of dignity.

He returned to the cool interior of the St. James and its bar, where his old companions sat for another drink. It was not a habit in which he usually indulged, but the separate occasions of the day earned him such self-indulgence.

She decided it was best he lie still, with the heavy draperies closed to keep out as much noise as possible. She would shut the door also, for the same reason. And to ensure this time that he remained in the safety of his room and did not wander the hallways without her guidance.

She would talk to Diaz and scold him, demand that he not allow Mr. Mitchell to have such an adventure again. Not until she determined it was in his best interest.

The exercise had not been good for her patient. As he lay quiet under her hands, she could feel his heart pound in the confines of his chest. His head moved away from her gaze, and his eyes were closed as if to deny her even that small pleasure, a glimpse of their color, a sense of what he was feeling. He seemed to suffer a new modesty from her touch, as if he could not bear her woman's hands on him. He must know the damage he'd done, yet he would not apologize in any manner as she fussed over him and talked to him as if he were a child.

Now he slept, hard, like in the beginning of his illness

when she often did not know if he were alive or dead. At times his chest barely moved until she had to bend down and feel the breath come from his mouth to reassure herself.

How could he do this to her? He had frightened her so, standing in the hall, bare-legged, barefooted, hanging on Martin Smith like a street urchin. There had been defiance in his stance and deliberate mockery in his accepting Mr. Smith's help but not her own.

She was wounded by her patient, her soul ached, and her heart saddened. She crossed her hands beneath her bosom and could pretend to feel its fluttering. She could not help herself. He was truly beautiful to her, only her. Long and thinned, skin yellow from illness, blue eyes closed against intruders, hands weak and motionless on the cotton blanket.

She pulled a chair close to the bed and sat down heavily. Her hands reached out independent of her will and took one of her patient's hands, holding it gently, pressed between her fingers. The contrast was unnerving; his skin was dark with years of work, the knuckles raised, one finger bent oddly and scarred at the tip. When she turned his hand over, the stark whiteness of the palm surprised her, as if she had not seen a hand such as this before.

The hands of a working man, hardened, toughened by life. Lela Miller began to cry. She raised the limp hand to her mouth, kissed the center of the palm, and saw her tears fall on the dry skin. She was shamed by reawakened feelings and caught still in their power.

So beautiful, so young; dependent on her for his healing. Blinded, lost, struggling to regain his life.

She kissed the hand again and again, until the slight twitch of muscle along the arm startled her. She pressed her cheek against the back of the hand, marveling at the smell, knowing his touch even as he slept.

It was a dream out of exhaustion. The woman was beautiful, long hair unbound, dark eyes, red lips. He could not focus on her face, but she was beautiful. Her touch soothed and aroused him. She stroked his chest, kissed his hand, and he

115

could not reach for her. He was bound, a prisoner, teased by her scent, her voice, the warmth of her body.

Lights flashed inside his eyes; liquid shapes moved in darkness, formed and re-formed new colors he could see. His head ached, and his mouth held only dust. Skin pressed his skin, bone traced his bone, heat matched his own, drawing from him his last energy.

With a supreme effort Blue grabbed for the enemy. He caught mounds of flesh, squeezed, heard a soft moan. Sweetness overwhelmed him as he fought his dream come alive. A voice began to ease him, a new melody that rocked him into sleep.

He hurt her with those strong hands. He crushed her breast, and she did not mind. The touch inflamed her, bringing with it memories of her dead husband she had tried not to keep.

Her cowboy's face lacked all color, and the mouth was drawn, bloodless, the eyes clenched shut. Lela Miller knew she loved him then. He needed her as no one ever had. Even Thomas Miller with his acceptance and laughter, his taking her in the marriage bed, even as he stood up for her and proclaimed his love, he would sometimes glance away, as if a full view of her homely face and cow's body was too much for him.

Her cowboy did not see the thin hair and watery eyes, the lumpy travesty of a woman's form. He touched the heart of her, her bosom and belly, her wide hips meant for children. He touched her blindly, with restless hands, and she did not retreat from the contact.

He reached for her even in his sleep, and she loved him in return.

THIRTEEN

GRANT FORMAN AND Homer Nelson were in the bar. They acknowledged Smith only with a raised glass and slight nod. Smith was grateful to sit down with little fuss and was embarrassingly eager for his first sip of brandy. He watched his hand shake as he raised the glass and used that failing as an excuse to gulp the liquor in one swallow. He accepted another drink and forced himself to only sip it. But the fire had already spread through his belly, and its warmth steadied him. Finally he was able to relax. These men were his friends.

Forman spoke up casually. "Heard that boy a your'n tried taking a walk. He's a lot tougher than old Farmer figured." Martin nodded, thinking once again that word spread fast in a small town. But there was more on Forman's mind. "What you plannin' to do with a blind rider, Martin? Not much good to no one that way. What in hell can you do, but I reckon you owe him somethin'."

In that short statement Grant Forman drew in all of Martin's worries and concerns. Then Homer butted in, offering his bit of information. "Heard 'bout that surveyor feller, sounded good. Damn good, you might say." Homer didn't break a smile, but Martin nodded to the choice of words. "Not ol' Grant here, he's of a mind there ain't no way to fool nature. Me, I'm thinkin' that a few rocks and a bit of wall and we got that water corraled and waitin' on us. This round anyway."

117

Martin looked at his drinking companions. Forman wasn't much one way or the other. Lean, bald, face half burned brown by the sun, half-white from hiding under a wide-brimmed hat. Looked like what he was, a rancher worked hard all his life.

Homer, though, he was different. He stood five feet five or less in boots and didn't seem much taken on the notion he was shorter than the rest of the world. He sat in a big chair toward the back of Lambert's bar, and his feet didn't quite reach the floor. And there he was, talking on the dam and the new plans for irrigation, and grinning at Martin and Grant over the rim of his glass, wagging his head sideways, allowing them time to appreciate the wit of his words.

Then he got going again; nothing could stop Homer when he had the wind up in him. "Now Grant here, he thinks the world stays the same, no vision, no lookin' ahead. You, Martin, I 'spect you been studyin' that survey and been figurin' and checkin', awonderin' how. That right, Martin?"

The faces turned toward him, and two hands were raised in a salute. Martin refilled his glass and joined them. His friends, good friends, a true blessing to a man.

Homer went on as if the silent exchange were only a hesitation in his continuing tale. "Lot happenin' in this town, Martin. Them mines playin' out, that's bad luck. Buckminster, now he's a pure fool. And a bad 'un. Got a burr in him gall a man twice his size. He blames you, Martin, for his fool luck. Best be careful, that one ain't much given to kindness."

The three friends sipped the liquor, thought their own thoughts in the company of good friends. And Homer got started again, miserable as usual with too much quiet. "You know Jose, sheepman over by Springer's place. He come by this mornin', lookin' for coffee and beans. Told me a wild tale, figured at first was pure foolish but then, you might be wantin' to know this 'un, Martin.

"Now Jose, he said he was lookin' for a ewe strayed off, feared she was took by a coyote. Anyway, he got down by the river and saw somethin' strange. Figured you got to know, seein' it's about your child.'' Martin sat up and put the glass of brandy down. ''Now Jose, he said he saw a girl ridin' a bay looked like that Texas pony a your'n. Said no way you couldn't miss it was a girl, no disrespect meant, Martin. Just tryin' to repay me for the coffee. Said he thought it was your child, gallopin' near the river, jumpin' a downed tree. Made it sound a pretty picture, but he said it was your child. And she was wearin' pants. Men's pants.''

It fitted, Martin thought. She had not bothered to change that evening. She had brought him his whiskey and smiled enchantingly, and they had both avoided speaking about her scandalous clothes.

Each part of his world was coming undone—his wife, now his child. An itinerant horse tamer and a wolfer turned speculator. Whatever the gods had in store for him next, Martin Smith prayed it would come quick and soon. He was tired.

Homer went on as if there had been no silent interruption. ''Martin, what you plannin' about the dam? And Buckminster? Mines, too, while I'm askin'. We gonna have a lot a men wanderin' the street that can't do nothin' but bring trouble. Like when ol' Maxwell, he sold out to them English, and the settlers tried to pick up his land. Men walkin' 'round, talkin' big words 'bout their rights when all they was wantin' was what belonged to another man. Don't want to go back to those times, no sir. We sure don't.''

Grant Forman grunted something that sounded like agreement, but the noise did not deter Homer from his ramblings. ''Weren't that Buckminster a friend of McMains's? Takin' after his old buddy, it sure looks like. Blamin' anyone else but himself for his failure. What you think, Martin?''

Homer didn't much care there was no answer. The heart of his question was too close to Martin Smith's despair for him to talk. The failings of mankind did little for pleasant solitude and a glass of brandy shared with friends.

Then there was the question of Flora, out in the open now with the sheepherder's tale. She had been brought up a lady and now took to wearing men's pants and racing a Texas pony. And she had knelt in the dirt beside the injured cowboy, hands covered with his blood, unmindful of the filth and manure. His child had changed into a woman, and he had not realized it until now.

Then there was a time when he had seen Flora in young Mitchell's company, and when she came to the house, her face was flushed and the light in her eyes was different, far-away and shining.

He made a connection that startled and disgusted him. His own daughter could not behave like a street girl. She could not have taken a fancy to the horse tamer, not that awkward man full of strange action and wild humor. She was born and raised a lady, intended for better things.

"You all right, Martin?" It was Homer, patient, legs swinging gently above the distant floor.

"No problem, Homer, just thinking." His Elizabeth had been a lady, and she had taken to bedroom matters quite nicely. When it was necessary, she had tended horribly wounded men and even drove a team, helped round up strayed cattle. Through it all she maintained her poise and her beauty, her air of manners. Yet the same Elizabeth had loved his body and their joined pleasure, and she had borne him a child who looked, and acted, just like her.

It waited for him, convenient if unorthodox, a solution that would raise a few eyebrows and start a few stories but would keep his child home, in the shadow of her father. Still in her father's care, as her husband was blind.

He would not imagine his Flora in bed with the man; he would not see her touched by those work-roughened hands. There would be a price to pay for his misuse of the cowboy, but he did not have to see all its complexities.

Martin Smith poured himself a new brandy. Both his companions refused the refill. The absolute truth stared straight at him; for all his wealth and land now, he had come to this country with nothing but a willingness to work hard and take risks. He was no better then, or now, than Blue Mitchell, no more educated or refined. He had learned, so could Mitchell.

He respected the man, even more after his attempt to guide the man on his stubborn quest. There had been humor in

Mitchell's voice when he explained his plight, and an unexpected grace. Even in the ungainly nightshirt Mitchell possessed inherent dignity. His daughter, married to the likes of Blue Mitchell; there could be worse waiting for his Flora, much worse.

He was definitely unsteady when he stood up and put his empty glass down on the table. The bottle of brandy stood there in solitary grandeur. It was almost empty. Martin's hand was not accurate when he divided the remaining liquor into the three glasses, but his friends drank with him when he raised his glass in silent toast.

They were good enough friends to understand and did not ask what they were saluting; Martin Smith toasted the marriage of Flora Elizabeth Smith and one Blue Mitchell.

He couldn't borrow a nickel, not five pennies, not even the makings for a smoke. No one gave him nothing. Not a "good morning" or afternoon or whatever time it was. Folks in town saw him coming and shuffled off, changed direction and disappeared.

Word was out—Albert Buckminster lost it all, gone bad. Broke, useless, used up.

He was dead inside, now that the liquor couldn't burn away the damage. Dead where thoughts and old plans and yearnings formed his broken defense against the world of reality.

A dead man walking upright, like a mortally wounded grizzly bear.

It weren't a pretty picture, and it sure weren't a nice place. Buckminster was lost, beaten by the cards and the turn of fate, beaten by an old man who rode a chestnut mare.

Buckminster went back to the wolf he'd once come into the country to hunt down. He was worth less than a ten-dollar bounty pinned on his ravaged, flea-bitten hide. The horse he still owned, the damnable roan mare, wouldn't sell for enough to cover her feed. The gold nugget hugged to his belly with its rawhide string was less than a few dollars in coin value. A rotten leather pouch held a sample of gold dust, his saddle had a broken tree, and the bit and bridle were rusted and patched.

If the truth be known, if the facts got let out, Albert Buckminster weren't worth a fart in a high wind. Cold broke and tired. Goddamn.

Buckminster rubbed his belly with cold hands. He needed a drink and a woman, and then revenge. He wanted the hide off Martin Smith. He wanted a bottle of Lambert's good whiskey. A woman's warm flesh under him, a woman's smell to excite him.

Goddamn!

FOURTEEN

THIS TIME WHEN he heard a sound and rolled his head toward it, he could almost see a shadow moving toward him. The sound translated into a door opened, footsteps on the hard wood.

He half sat up, opened his mouth to tell her, and then shut it. He could hear the intake of breath and knew Mrs. Miller was already worrying about what was wrong. He wasn't going to talk about shadows with her; she'd fuss and drive him half-mad. He quickly lay back down and shut his eyes hard.

He'd been lying in bed thinking, rested after a long sleep. Been quite a morning, he thought. Walking felt good, taking care of himself. Even if he didn't make it all the way back to his room, he had a start on getting better.

He'd been puzzling over the identity of his nurse until she came into the room, and this time, when she spoke his name, her face and story jumped right there in front of him.

The funny little man, Thomas Miller, and his mail-order bride. The stories run through town, first mocking the newlyweds, then talking love and wedded bliss and then stopping short when Miller took sick and died.

Blue had never met the bride, never been to town when she walked through. He'd heard the stories about her ugliness, heard all the jokes. But she didn't sound ugly to Blue at all.

"Mr. Mitchell?" Soft-voiced, gentle, as if not to disturb him but to let him know she was nearby. "Mr. Mitchell, if you want, I can bring up a meal for you. You've slept through noon, but I know you must be hungry, with all the exercise of this morning."

There was a sad note in her voice, and Blue wondered, then guessed maybe she didn't want him acting on his own. Not like this morning. Not at all. She'd fed and bathed him, held him while he was feverish. He didn't answer her question but rolled his head back and kept his eyes closed.

There was a moment of no sound, and then a hand took his, and through half-opened eyes he could watch the silhouette of his arm lift in the air. There was a whisper of breath on the back of his hands, and he blushed furiously, mortally embarrassed. The woman had kissed his hand. Mitchell pretended to be asleep. They would both be offended if he awakened now from his pretense and caught her in the act.

She was pure lonely. The thought comforted him. Lonely and widowed, a big, homely woman in a small town that talked too much, and Thomas Miller had brought her here and left her too quickly. Blue was rigid, motionless. Shocked by what he was thinking, about loneliness and comfort and needs.

Then Martin Smith's daughter appeared in his mind, a picture of her pretty face, a memory of her body pushed against his, while the big woman held his hand and stroked his arm, caressed his shoulders across his chest. He tasted the daughter's mouth, felt her thin bones, and smelled her special heat, but it was Lela Miller's hands that touched him.

His imagination filled him, and he almost didn't hear the faint voice at the doorway ask its question and break the spell. It was the breed kid; he knew by the accent. "Señora, there is work for me, yes?"

The woman's shape shifted and moved, his hand was gently laid by his side, and the back of his hand was cold now. He feathered his eyelids and could make out sizes, colors, mostly gray and light yellow, almost sunlight.

He could see. And if he forced his eyes to focus, his head

ached badly and his heart pounded. But he could see, and that let him smile before he coasted back into a dreamless sleep.

The roan mare was well into middle years and suffered badly from neglect. She had been with the sorrel gelding for five years and fought the change back to a saddle horse.

Buckminster's weight as he hauled himself into the old saddle did not help the mare's temper. She would have cow-kicked or bucked to show displeasure, but that took energy, and Longacre had been feeding her minimum rations on the unpaid bill.

The hostler had watched Buckminster catch and saddle the roan, and he held out his hand for payment due. If there had not been two men waiting, eager to rent horses, Buckminster would have given out what Longacre deserved, but he was careful and paid a bit of the gold dust and made a new promise. Longacre shook his head, and took the gold, and bad-mouthed Buckminster as soon as his back was turned. He knew, even though he could not hear the words. The two men laughed when the old man spoke, and Buckminster knew what that meant. He raged inside and filed the old man's intended insult away until he could use it.

It was late afternoon, and he had no real destination. Hot, windy, small dust devils whirled through town, spooking horses, drawing ladies' skirts around their fine legs.

Buckminster goaded the mare until she broke into a lumbering trot. He hung on the saddle horn and felt the broken tree jab into him. The roan threw her head, and Buckminster slapped her with the reins. The mare balked, and her rider lashed at her with reins and spur. A woman coming out of a store saw him and raised her hand, called a name loudly, and Buckminster kicked the mare hard enough for her to bleed.

The mare gave in, trotted forward and then broke into an awkward gallop. She shied at a corner, where a skirt rose high to expose white petticoats. Buckminster unraveled then, as if the frayed cord that held him to civilization had been cut. He raised his quirt and swung it on the mare's head. She shied and leaped sideways, and Buckminster hit her again. Blood sprayed from the wound, and Buckminster licked his lips, tasted the hot salt, and smelled the raw, sweet taste.

The mare tried to spin, but the curb bit tore at her tongue. The mare slowed, and Buckminster whipped her mercilessly. She galloped on, through the attack from her rider, running blindly along the length of the river.

Free of town, free of the eyes of civilization, Buckminster laced the mare until red foam coated her, and even through the beating she slowed from her first burst of speed to a jagged trot, then a slow walk. Then the mare stopped, legs quivering, sides heaving. Buckminster guessed he'd killed her where she stood, and let his feet slip from the stirrups, waiting for her to go down.

The mare took a deep breath and reared, and Buckminster slid off her back and hit the hard ground. Half-stunned, he lay quiet as the mare kicked out in anger and trotted toward the river and green grass.

He tasted dust, heard ringing, and tried to follow the sound of the truant mare, but he was too tired. He lay there, on the packed road, perfectly still, arms and legs spread out, head uncovered. The late sun bothered his eyes, and his nose itched, the hand clenched around the quirt ached, and he sat up, looked around. Empty sky, low sun, trees casting long shadows. Birds, a horse whinnying far away; nothing bothered with Albert Buckminster.

When he stood, his right ankle buckled under him and he fell, stood again and limped cautiously to a nearby tree. He leaned back, licked his dry lips clean, and absently looked at his boot. A nail stuck out where the heel should have been. He cursed the mare soundly, dug out the nail with his knife, and was more careful when he tried to walk again. It was awkward, to balance without the boot heel, but he was not injured by the fall.

He tracked the mare for a short distance and saw her trail head off toward the lush grass of the river's edge. And he laughed when he heard the sounds, like a grizzly caught in a trap, snorting, stamping, bushes rustling. The damned mare got herself tangled, caught herself up for Buckminster, so he wouldn't have to chase her.

He followed her tracks into the brush and found her. He stood back and laughed at the sight. Her head was caught at her knees, hung on short reins jammed in a branch. The mare scented her tormenter and rolled her eyes and tried to kick. Her bowels loosened in panic, and her reaction pleased Buckminster. He'd made his mark on the damned mare.

He hit her rump, and she slammed into the small trees of her prison, whipping herself in a frenzy to escape. Her age beat her, and she sagged and quit. The roan mare stood with her head near her knees and waited. Buckminster grinned. He was going to enjoy this.

But when he released his knife from its sheath, stepped toward the mare, and actually grabbed the broken reins, she could not give in to the final assault. She reared back, found unexpected freedom, and swung around, leaped forward and slammed into a solid tree. The sound of her neck breaking was all Buckminster could hear. She had ultimately defeated him.

He had to pick his way to the corpse, bending down to avoid the strong branches, the stout tangle of limbs and old brush. When he shoved the dead mare with his boot, the flesh was already bloated and stiff. He kicked her several times, until a chattering behind him unnerved him. He looked back, then quickly came around to see a large bird resting on a limb. Another bird joined the first, and then another. Buckminster cursed them, then drew his pistol out and pantomimed shooting.

The biggest of the birds eyed him but did not move. Two others rose leisurely at the mock threat. Buckminster laughed, cocked the pistol, and sighted down the barrel, targeting the biggest bird's skinny neck. A good day for hunting. He eased back the trigger and felt the pressure go from his finger up his arm, deep into his bruised chest. Satisfaction at last. He let the hammer fall, heard the loud click, and saw the bird's bright knowing eye laugh at him.

Empty, by God, out of shells. Not reloaded after the last

time. He threw the gun at the bird. The pistol skipped on the trunk of the tree and fell into sand. The bird clicked its beak, baiting Buckminster for his neglect.

The other two birds circled and settled back in the tree. The biggest of the trio stretched its neck out, blinked its red eyes, and ruffled its feathers. Buckminster stalked the base of the tree, picked up his pistol, and tried to wipe the sand from it. He gave up and put it back in the holster. The birds ignored him, and he could not reach them without a weapon.

The mare was a mound of already rotting flesh. Buckminster stood in the shade and stared at the dead animal. The birds stared along with him, willing to outwait their one competitor.

It was then that Buckminster realized he was on the road to Smith's Broken S. That's where he was going on this ride, out to talk with Smith, settle things with him, straighten out the troubles before they got out of hand. And now here he was, stranded, watching a dead horse.

First the mine, then the loan and now the mare. A good animal, still valuable, rugged enough to pull a wagon and well trained to ride. A valuable animal, dead. Martin Smith, dead. Smith's image ingrained in his mind; standing on the St. James's steps; summer sun, heat, old trees' scant shade. The old man who destroyed Buckminster's plans.

There wasn't much point in his efforts, but Buckminster grabbed the head of the dead roan mare and yanked at the bridle. The yellowed teeth grinned at him, the rubbery lips drawn back in the final joke. The bridle hung on one ear, and he couldn't get it free. He raised the skull. An eye blinked at him, and he cried out. The headstall leather parted, and the bit clanked against the dried teeth. Buckminster knelt in a clump of trees and brush, next to the corpse of a useless mare, a rotted bridle hanging from his hand. He stood up, kicked the skull, and cursed until the trio of hungry birds rose from their perch.

The saddle was no better. Buckminster rubbed his butt where the tree had gouged him. The rope was frayed, the stirrups rusted. He took the saddle bags and threw out the leaky canteen, but kept the half-chewed blanket for warmth. The evening would turn cool.

When he stood in the middle of the road, he knew the extent of his actions. He'd been here before, not long ago, due to Martin Smith's actions. But then he had a roan mare and a limping sorrel worth a few dollars to the greedy. Now there was truly nothing left of him.

The weight of his remaining saddle gear was a burden and a reminder. He nodded to an unspoken word, heard clearly the listing of his own actions that had brought him back to walking a dusty road.

His mind refused to accept that responsibility. It was not Albert Buckminster who made the mistakes; it was others, any others who came into his range of view. He would not take on this new disaster, no one but a fool would choose to keep living with such mistakes.

It was Martin Smith and Frank and Charles Springer— they were his tormentors. The rising fury rocked him, tumbled him where he stood, he fought for his balance on the packed earth, rocked by unleashed anger.

He refused the truth. He was bigger, stronger, and smarter, and the world did not like him for his strengths. They cut him down to their puny size, and now they would find the terrible truth about Albert Buckminster.

He left the roan mare and the gear he had stripped from her corpse; there would be much more waiting for him. No one could stop him. The climb from the stand of trees back to the road strained his bruised muscle and bone. He added the pain to his list. He stared down the road toward the miserable town, then he looked right, toward Smith's kingdom, which rightly belonged to him.

Dust threaded along the river, rising high, moving fast and trailing off. Horses, perhaps, and team and wagon, coming for him, a lift into town. He waited impatiently, rubbing his face and neck, tasting dryness, exhaustion, and banked anger. Hunger purged even the anger. He needed a ride into town, a good meal, and a long sleep. Past that he didn't much care.

The dust came closer, two dark heads bobbed in a quick

pace, and wheels squeaked and whistled. A wagon, a good team; he was saved.

The team spooked where the dead horse was hidden, and Buckminster admired the skill of the woman who held the lines and deftly handled the nervous horses. He walked toward her. It was not a ranch vehicle but more of a fine lady's runabout. A woman drove; by God, a woman came to his rescue! Old hungers rose, old needs unsatisfied. Buckminster's step quickened, his senses on edge.

By God, it was the Smith girl come to get him. The team was those part-Morgans the old man bragged on, ears pricked, heads naturally set high, tails plumed; they were a pretty sight for a tired man.

There was justice left in the world. Buckminster removed his hat, taught once of the social observances, aware of them even in God's abandoned country. "Miss, you come at the right time. My miserable . . . my old mare took off, and I need a ride to town. Thank you, miss. Most appreciated."

She stared at him and then tipped the buggy whip, poked a bundle resting beside her on the narrow seat. Her voice wavered, but she was a determined little thing. "Mr. Buckminster, I can send someone out from town, but as you can see there is no room in the buggy. I am taking these things into town, for a friend. A sick friend. There just isn't room."

A mere girl got up with airs way above her, too fancy for the likes of Buckminster. Just junk in the buggy seat, a saddle rolled up and tied, a pair of tall boots, chaps with silver on each leg; cowboy gear riding in the buggy and no room for a man like Buckminster.

He stepped toward the girl, intending to discard the gear and make room for his bulk. She misread his intentions, for she raised the whip and the team took notice. Both horses snorted and rolled their eyes, and when the whip flicked above them, they decided it was meant for a command. In perfect unison the team stepped into a high trot and came right at Buckminster.

By God, he weren't afraid, but he got out of the way and heard the girl shout at him, "I'll send someone back for

130

you.'' As if she were taunting him, as if she didn't know there weren't a man in the world would offer an act of friendship to Buckminster now. Too much jealousy, too much hatred.

He began to walk in the trail of settling dust. And the anger came back, rolled up in hunger and weariness. He coughed and spit, wiped his chin. Hungry, by God, and no coin to match his need.

There wasn't much waiting for him in Cimarron, but it was better than nothing. And he wasn't going to let the sons of bitches beat him now.

FIFTEEN

SHE WORE A dress, her father's favorite, of soft rose flowers cut demurely at the throat, only just revealing her slender figure. Flora was careful to pick out the right dress and asked Peter Charley to harness the team of Morgans.

She had not liked the look in Peter Charley's eyes when she spoke to him, but it was nothing she could explain or fuss about, no insult or mis-said word. But there had always been a sense with Peter Charley that he knew the thoughts in her private mind and did not approve of them.

There was no reason for her to care what a mission-taught Indian thought about her. Except that he had become a friend, of sorts, to Blue Mitchell. And Flora did care what that young man thought about her.

Her father's questions over the past day or so began the connection in her mind, and then her dreams at night, her waking thoughts, put it together. Now she intended to drive into Cimarron and take over her duties as Blue's nurse.

Did she love Blue Mitchell? She did not understand the question; she dreamed of the man, tasted him, felt his body. Awakened alone in her narrow child's bed she sobbed and ached and went to sleep again, dreaming of Blue Mitchell.

Perhaps that was love. She truly did not know. But when her father asked his sly questions, she knew enough not to tell him the extent and vividness of her feelings and her dreams. No father, no matter how much he valued honesty, would choose to hear such words from his daughter.

Papa had suddenly turned old, she thought. Gray and tired, his eyes runny and moist, his hands constantly rubbing together. He was cold, he told her, but it was no matter, not important. Then he would cough and discreetly spit into a fine white handkerchief, and the sound was dry and aching.

The night he had come home and found her wearing man's pants he had said nothing. Her papa was getting old. She watched him that night, saw him turn and walk away from her, back bowed, white hair standing away from his skull. Walking like an old man walked.

It was then she decided to see Blue Mitchell. And using the excuse of bringing him the familiarity of his gear occurred to her as she dressed and readied herself.

The gear was stored in the adobe shack used for harness and nails, shoes for the horses, medicines for various illnesses. The temptation was to go through the rolled blanket and the heavy saddlebags, but the men were watching her. Not obviously—they rarely stared directly at her. But they watched and waited, and she was intimidated by their knowing eyes.

Peter Charley himself stood at the head of the team and held them while Flora climbed gracefully into the buggy and settled herself. He stared directly at her, and this time he nodded almost in approval. "Miss, that Mitchell's tough. Not one to fool himself. You taking him the gear might be a starting place for him. You doing right, miss. Be careful."

She was quickly conscious of two things at once; her mouth hung open and her face was flushed, hot, reddening from the half compliment. Never had this man spoken so to her. Never before had it mattered.

Flora was gracious enough to smile shyly at Peter Charley before taking the lines and directing the team toward the road along the river. It would be good for Blue to rub his fingers along the lines of his saddle, smell the stale sweat of the blanket, roll the fine weaving of the horsehair bridle between two hands and hear the bell of the bit chains.

He would take small comfort from these things now, and then discard them, go to his next role. The word was inescapable; he was blind. Dr. Farmer said it was permanent. The woman whom Papa hired to nurse him, she would walk gently around that fact and talk as if a light waited for Blue. Flora knew that much, and she also knew Blue would not ask for protection. There had never been a woman's softness to protect him; he would not want that type of protection now.

What Flora was planning would be outwardly cruel, but it was the beginning of getting Blue for herself.

She struggled with the team; the saddle bounced on the narrow seat, and the stirrups rubbed her thigh. Twice she tried to push the gear away and keep the team at a steady trot. But the road was badly rutted, and the saddle leaned into her. She was hampered by the long, full skirt of the pretty rose dress and wished for the plain comfort of pants and a shirt, a long duster. But this time she wanted to be a lady for Blue, even if he could not see her.

It was then that the team acted bad and were hard to handle, and as Flora fought them, the horrible man rose up in front of her. Give him a ride, allow that fat body to sit next to her on the seat. She knew better; there was no point in pretending even the basics of politeness.

He frightened her, with his greasy clothes and wrinkled, red face. The eyes never looked straight at her, the hands always seemed ready to reach out and take. Her offer to send help was a sham. She knew as well as he did that no one in Cimarron would go out of their way for him. He made no friends, felt himself to be superior, and brutalized those who would socialize with him.

She was relieved to let the team move out as fast as they chose. She wanted only to get far away from the terrible, hulking man who stared at her.

The breed child came out and took the team for Flora. The Morgans were still excited; Flora had let them run, and they were white with foam, steaming sweat, eager to run again.

Papa had warned her not to run them without good cause as they were hot-blooded and temperamental. The thought of that fat man walking the road behind her was reason enough for Flora.

When the team calmed enough to stand, the child helped drag the gear out of the buggy. Flora directed him and told him to carry the bundles to Blue's room. She corrected herself quickly, saying "Señor Mitchell's room," but the child was not stupid, and those eyes of his watched her carefully and seemed to find something of importance in her face.

She chose to carry the saddle, while Diaz followed with the rest; the blanket and the lovely bridle, the bags stuffed with clothing and books, an old slicker, a sheepskin coat mended too many times. It was not much for one man's life.

Flora stopped on the landing and looked out the window. The late sun exposed the dusty street that divided Cimarron. With the particular light, it was almost beautiful. Behind her she could hear Diaz curse softly. She stared out the window, suddenly overwhelmed with what she was about to do. It could bring nothing but anger and sadness to an already helpless man.

With her eyes shut, she let her fingers rub the smooth leather of the saddle. Shaped in her fist, the horn rose from the cantle, a rope hung from the off side. She caressed the metal horn, touched the worn seat, and brought her fingers to her face, blindly smelling the faint odors. The cure of leather, the distant taste of salt. Dulled metal, twisted hemp.

That was all; no motion, no distance, no green trees or light. They waited for her when she opened her eyes. They were denied forever to the gear's owner. Tears swelled in her eyes, and her throat ached from a silent cry.

Footsteps came toward the landing, heavy sounds, closing in on a sightless girl. Flora opened her eyes and saw the big woman known as Mrs. Miller. She came out of the shadows, awkward in a shapeless calico dress, thin hair wrapped in a bandanna, hands reddened and chapped. Flora knew this was the gargoyle guarding Blue's sickroom. Papa had hired her.

135

"Mrs. Miller, I am Flora Smith. Papa thought it would be best to put Blue's gear in his room. It will give him comfort while he recovers. Papa thought . . ." A small lie, but the woman loomed over Flora, and she felt she needed her father's command to back her up. The woman was nothing more than a hired nurse, after all, and had little say in what was done to the invalid.

But Mrs. Miller did not seem to be deceived. "Child, I do not think it wise for Mr. Mitchell to have more visitors today. He is exhausted, and it is getting toward supper time. There are no provisions for visitors; the room is quite small. And there certainly is no place for that smelly gear in the room of a sick man."

She looked past Flora to the boy carrying the rest of Blue's things and spoke abruptly to him. "Diaz, you take that downstairs and put it in a storage room. We certainly do not want to upset Mr. Mitchell any more than necessary." As if Flora did not count, as if Mrs. Miller's word was law.

Diaz stood on the top step before the landing, burdened with smelly coats and heavy bags, and watched the two women with great admiration. They were fighting for a man, that Blue Mitchell. A blinded cowboy with no money, no work, nothing left.

Diaz shook his head, awed by what men and women could do for each other. He could not help but see the fine shape of the younger woman; she was only inches from him. Her hips were gently rounded, her hair flowed freely, and he could even smell a sweet perfume from her if he leaned forward only a bit.

Above her was the homely woman who tended the sick man. Washed and wiped him and sat with him. And who had fallen in love with him. Diaz was no fool; he had seen much of the world and judged it in terms of his survival. He was an accomplished survivor. Yet his battered heart went to the big señora, who loved without reason and without chance.

In the meantime, Diaz would stand on the step and make

no comment, draw no attention to himself. He would listen and watch the confrontation, and obey its winner.

He would bet on the girl, although she did not have the years. She had her papa and his power, and she had a beauty that would confuse and defeat Mrs. Miller. He would bet on the girl, and he would ache for the woman.

Flora took two steps, a small distance, but it brought her close to her opponent. The woman's size stopped her. Flora took her lower lip gently in her teeth and smiled. Gestures calculated to disarm her father and enchant any man. They were the basis of her arsenal.

Mrs. Miller was not interested. "Miss, think of what you are doing. He cannot see, and you wish to tease him with what he can no longer have. That is cruel, and I cannot believe it of your father that he could choose such a course of action. I forbid it."

Both combatants were surprised by the strength of the words. Flora actually stepped back, and Mrs. Miller frowned, her watery eyes wide and vulnerable.

It was the sight of that homely face that gave Flora new courage. She pushed past Mrs. Miller as if the woman did not exist, and headed toward what she guessed was the sick room. Diaz did not follow, nor did he pick up the saddle where the girl dropped it. But she did not know this and assumed that he was close behind with all the gear. Mrs. Miller be damned; she would do what she wanted.

But the big woman moved fast and was quite literally in the way when Flora found the right room. Arms folded across her jutting bosom, she was pure intimidation, and Flora suddenly lost her boldness.

The two women stared at each other coldly, any pretense at civilized behavior given way to primitive battle. Flora prettily wiped her hands on her face, drew up that sweet smile, and let the ugly lady have the full effect of her words. "I insist, Mrs. Miller. I am doing what my father wishes. And it is he who pays your salary. You will step aside, and Diaz will bring the gear." She turned around, and the stupid boy was still on the landing, waiting. It made her angry that he had not come with her, and she let the force of that anger out on Mrs. Miller.

"Blue does not belong to you. He is my father's hired hand, and I am here now to care for him. You are no longer needed."

There were no other words that could destroy Lela Miller as completely as those the young girl spoke to her. Her only value in life was to be needed, as she would rarely be loved or desired. And now this slip of a girl found the weak place and speared it with her quick tongue. Lela Miller bowed her head and wiped her moist eyes, completely beaten by a much younger adversary. She accepted this defeat as she accepted all others, as part of God's plan for her. To temper her soul on this earth until her time of release had come.

Lela Miller stepped aside, back touched to the door frame, eyes cast down, hands folded meekly across her skirt. There was nothing now for her but to look one more time at the face and form of Blue Mitchell, and then leave.

She stood patiently, forgotten by her conqueror. And she did not even bother to look up as the breed kid, Diaz, slid past her into the small room. He was all but hidden under his great smelly burden, and a brief flash of anger smothered Lela Miller. It was wrong, to taunt her patient with his lost past, and to take him from her without warning or compassion.

She could no longer bear her surroundings and wished to be outdoors, in air not tasting of sickness and defeat.

Diaz obeyed the señorita's orders, but his heart went with the señora.

Blue heard the noise, the commotion, and half sat up, blinked his eyes and rubbed them hard. Even the smell was strange, close to familiar but out of place. The outline in the doorway was not the big woman, Mrs. Miller. But it was a woman— that he knew from the scented soap, the rustle of clothing, and the lighter step.

He strained to figure it out, twisting toward new sounds, aware of the figure coming much closer. When a soft hand

138

touched his face and the arm brushed his cheek, he sighed deeply. "Miss Flora, that you?"

It was a shock for her; he was blind yet called her name. She had said no more than the few words to the kid where to put down the gear. Flora quickly knew it would be easy to underestimate Blue Mitchell. And he kept at it, asking questions that revealed his mind.

"What you got there, Miss Flora? Smells like horses. You didn't bring one of your pa's good thoroughbreds up to cheer some, now did you? Wouldn't be a bad idea, ain't touch hide or hoof in some time." Then he sat up and turned his head toward a different sound. "That's my rig, ain't it, got my boots? Anything left of my hat . . . ?" Here the bravado left him and his voice turned quiet. "That damned . . . that colt, he come down hard on me."

As if he remembered too clearly, a spasm crossed his face and Flora hoped it was only the dark shading of the room. She did not want to witness self-pity, especially not in one she had made into a hero.

Then he confounded her again by rubbing a fist in one eye and then the other and shaking his head as if to clear his sight. "I maybe can't see nothing, Miss Flora, but I sure can smell that old saddle. Diaz, that you?"

Diaz was rooted to the spot; the head swiveled from the girl to him, and Diaz grasped the hat with both hands. It was uncanny, that blind eyes could find him. Not of the world, that a man once pronounced all but dead could sit up and talk like regular people and know what was brought to him, know where each stood and what was their burden.

Diaz dropped the hat, picked it up, and reverently placed it on a table so that the sweep of the brim was not flattened. The hat was stained and filthy, and there was a blot of dark crust that rose into the crown, but it was Blue Mitchell's hat.

"Thank you, Diaz. *Gracias*, hombre." With a short bow to the blind one who thanked him, Diaz fled from the room inhabited by demons.

Flora Smith watched the exchange, perplexed by words and actions she did not fully comprehend. But when Diaz

139

was finally gone, she drew a chair close to her man's bed and sat down. Blue wrestled with bed clothes, careful to have them up around his chest and shoulders, and sat up with his head rested against the wall. They began talking, their words overlapping in their hurry.

"Miss, I thank you for the visit. It ain't proper, or much comfort for you, watching a fool sitting in bed. So I thank you, 'specially for the gear, and won't mind you got to be going."

Her voice was softer, her manners better taught, so she knew better but talked on through his drawl anyway, impatient and curious. "You are much better. My papa said so. Dr. Farmer didn't think much of your chances, and Papa was discouraged, so I had to see for myself. Blue . . ."

She caught her breath, mindful suddenly of the few words her papa had spoken, the strange idea he had put in her mind. As she talked and watched the young man, she was again intrigued. The object of her curiosity was finally quiet, and she was able to fully satisfy her longing to truly see him for what he was.

It was a most intimate situation for an unchaperoned young lady. Perhaps she should have allowed poor Mrs. Miller to stay. The man was in bed and wore only a thin nightshirt to cover his nakedness. It was possible to follow the contours of his body beneath the light summer blanket, and startling images flooded Flora Smith's mind, causing her to blush hotly. She was relieved that the young man could not see her face.

But he lifted his hand and briefly touched his fingers to her own hand. As if he knew, as if he offered a gesture of sympathy, or pity.

So she talked to cover her confusion; she rambled on about the calf crop and the mine closings, how the mares were bred back and the foals well on their way. She thanked him for the manners of the Morgan team, although she did not admit to running them into town. And she told him that Peter Charley often asked how he was, and that her father gave him long explanations. When she spoke the Indian's name, she noted that Blue stiffened slightly and a strange look crossed his face. She would have asked him, but her mind was running and she could not stop.

Instead, she spoke of the chestnut filly, the first one he trained in the early spring. How her papa rode the filly and enjoyed her, and said that perhaps he would breed the filly to one of Charles Springer's stallions, and then next year, after the foal, Flora could have the mare for her own.

She didn't notice as she talked the exact moment when Blue's back slumped and his shoulders loosened, his head rolled back until his chin rested on his chest. She was intent on talking, terrified now that she was face-to-face with the man who was too often in her dreams.

Then the shadows in the room were impossibly long, and the big woman had not returned, and Flora knew it was past time for her to leave. She reasoned that when she left, Mrs. Miller would recover her common sense and complete her duties with her patient. She stood up and told Blue of her decisions. "I will send to the kitchen for your supper. That young man, Diaz, I believe you called him, will bring up the food and help you with . . . help you."

As she stood up and said her piece, Blue's head followed her body, as if he could truly see her.

A sadness marked her, swelling in her throat and causing her hands to rise together in a pious gesture. It was difficult to swallow, but she gallantly hid her feelings, as she had down throughout the interview, and smiled at her Blue even though he could not see her sweet good-bye. The smile would come through her words. "I am so glad, dear Mr. Mitchell. So glad to see you and to know you are well. I will come again in the morning to visit, and I will chide Mrs. Miller for her neglect."

She found the courage to capture one of his hands and bring it close to her face. The smell of him was intoxicating; even from a sickbed it was masculine and thrilling. He would come to the ranch, and she would take care of him. It was right. Papa would be so easy to convince.

"Good night, dear Mr. Mitchell."

141

SIXTEEN

THE ROCK HE sat on got hard real fast. Shifting his butt and cursing made no dent in the blasted surface. Finally Buckminster was forced to come to the conclusion that the damned girl had gone back on her word and no fool from town was coming out to give him a ride.

By God, he'd have to walk.

Two steps and he remembered the broken heel on his right boot. Goddamn. It took a sorry hand for such boots. He hated walking, but the dead mare left him no choice. That girl went back on her word and didn't send out a ride. He hated walking 'cause he was a big man in cowboy boots, one missing a heel, goddamnit, and he never put on miner's garb, not down to those fool shoes laced up and meant for a man on his feet. He was a mine owner, by God, not one who crawled down in a hole and picked at the rock, dug up what made others rich. He was an owner, not no worker for hire.

He was losing his hard-earned pattern of talk, going back to his growing up and forgetting how to put sounds that let him play with the powerful. He was losing hold and hated those pushing at him. By God, he was a mine owner, not a common cowhand.

All he'd needed was a loan on the Cutheart and a decent horse. Not much to ask, not much to expect, a man work as hard as he done, a man put his body into getting ahead, making a decent life.

Same with that damned girl and her fine buggy—all he needed was a little room on the seat, just that much to give him a ride.

All he needed was a bit of money, not much but enough that when he walked down the street folks stared and said, "There goes Albert Buckminster."

He didn't need much, just a few dollars and a ride into Cimarron.

Dirt scuffed up by his clumsy walk covered his legs and rose to make him cough. The back of his neck burned where the late sun hit him. His knees ached, and the heel of his right foot had a new blister. Walking, by God, where a man should have a horse. He sat down on a convenient log and finished his cursing.

Her retreat from the St. James was inglorious and humiliating, defeated by a spit of a girl. It was not fair, Lela Miller thought; it was never fair.

That young girl had not bathed the fever sweat from the patient, she had not guided his body over the pan to relieve his needs. She had not quite literally wiped his soiled bottom like a mewling babe new out of its mother. Yet she ordered Lela from the room, and those orders were to be obeyed.

The pain of the confrontation drove Lela Miller to act uncharacteristically. She left the safety of the St. James Hotel, where she had been needed for more than a month. She left the comfort of the small town streets and walked off an anger she had not felt before.

Few in the town looked up when she passed, few noticed her large shape or her lonesome destination. She walked quickly and was soon past the last buildings to mark the edge of town. Lela Miller paid no attention to her changing surroundings. Her mouth was dry in anger, her lips chapped. Her hands continuously rubbed each other in search of comfort and support. She did not know where she was going.

Her mind did not stop, did not cease its endless repetition of injustices; he was lost to her now, taken over by a pretty girl, seduced by a sweet false nature, a shapely bosom, a

143

clear skin, and a store-bought perfume. As if Flora Smith were a different category of female from poor Lela Miller, with her lumpy body and odd face. It was more than she could stand, to lose him as he was improving, talking to her, laughing and joking with her, becoming a friend, becoming an imagined lover.

It was more than a body could stand. Lela Miller walked on blindly. She did not look up from her thoughts, she did not see the fat man who was sitting on a rotting log. She had no notion of her impending confrontation with Buckminster.

The body and the farm woman's walk told him before he could see the features that it was Mrs. Miller. Who wouldn't give him a second chance, who wouldn't let a hand stray to her ample bosom or wide hip. Damned woman who got married out of a mail-order scheme and thought she was too good to talk with the likes of him.

Like the rest of the town, thinking they was a step above Albert Buckminster. He'd fool her. He'd make his manners and shame her.

What was her trouble; she jumped and screamed and put one of those big hands to her mouth when he stood up and bowed and called out her name. Like a true gentleman would. Did she think he was the devil come courting, or a wild savage lusting to scalp her? She weren't worth the fuss she was making. He stood his ground, though, ruined hat in his sweaty hands, eyes not quite focused on her face. If he didn't stare too close, she weren't that bad a looker. Good enough to keep him company, a woman at least. The female of the species.

Hell, he'd made his manners taking off his hat and such, even bowing from the waist like he'd seen; what'd she want, a lace hankie and a top hat?

He was hungry, but the pangs of missed meals were quickly replaced by an older, different, more primitive hunger. He tried to be polite; no one could say he didn't know his manners or didn't try to do things right.

"Evening, ma'am. Pleasure to see you out walking, a pleasure sure enough."

Now those weren't words to scare a lady, but this one sure jumped and turned pale if he was to look too close. Buckminster took a slow half step away from the woman, saw her trembling, and liked knowing it was on account of him. Being so close, close enough to touch. He hadn't touched a woman in a long time.

"Now, Mrs. Miller, ma'am, it's a right pleasure. I been lonely, like you are, ma'am."

She was already refusing him; he knew that from the clenched fists and the indrawn breath. Those fists were man-size, too, could do some damage. She was a stout woman, flattened him once with a fry pan and getting ready to do it again.

He searched his mind, he was too clever to get into a fight with a woman. Had to be some reason brought her this far from town and it almost dark. Then he put it together. "Why, I saw that pretty girl belong to Martin Smith, drive right by me 'bout an hour or so, driving that team right smart into town, seat all filled with cowboy gear and such. She must be a real pleasure for the cowboy to look at. Ah, I forgot he's blind, you been nursing him. Still, that Flora being his age and all, he must be enjoying his good fortune. I'm betting she was real smart, walked in and told you to get out and you had no choice. That ain't fair, ain't fair at all."

The big woman's hands let loose and her shoulders fell, and she would have fallen if Buckminster had not been right there to offer help. "Here, ma'am, you look cold. Let me help."

She was a-shaking and a-quivering like a new spring calf born late winter. And it weren't from no chill, he knew that. She was a woman married and bedded and quick-widowed, no matter how she looked, and she'd been tending to a man these past weeks all by herself, no one to see what she did. There were tears in the woman's eyes now, and Buckminster could bet on their source.

But the truth said out loud didn't get you what you wanted.

145

Lies worked better most times. Buckminster unrolled the smelly blanket pulled off the dead roan and offered it out like the finest beaver coat come from the fur trade. She stared at the offering as if it would likely bite. "Now, ma'am, you look cold to me. Let me help."

She jumped as if his outstretched hand were the fangs of a six-foot rattler. Kindness weren't going to work, he thought. He stepped in quick, grabbed the woman's arms, and held them tight to her sides. Pulled her close till he could smell the soap she used and taste the salt tears on her skin. She struggled and he liked it, liked her hips spread out for him, the heavy breasts pushed into his chest. She was a handful, and all of it female and struggling.

She pulled back, tripped and fell hard, and Buckminster let her go. She was quiet, laid out for him. He stood above her and grinned. She was liking this now, waiting for him.

He knelt over her. She kept still, eyes shut, mouth clamped; he drew up her skirt and yanked on the blouse until the buttons tore and the unbound, sagging breasts were exposed. He grunted almost in pain.

She was quiet, letting him fondle her. Accepting him like he knew she wanted to. Then a hand swept up with a rock, and the woman struck him hard on the skull. Buckminster stiffened and his mouth opened wide. His head rang with the pounding. For a short time he let go of the woman and tended to his head.

Before the woman could stand, before she could bunch her legs under her and get up and hit him again, Buckminster wrapped his two hands around her throat and killed her.

The last Lela Miller knew was the rank smell of Albert Buckminster and the world darkening around her.

Peter Charley found the body. It was early morning, just past false dawn, a restless time for him. He rode a small black mustang, a legacy. He always rode the black despite Mr. Smith's orders that he use the ranch cow ponies or the thoroughbreds. He rode the black, and when the restless feeling got him, he rode with only a blanket and a rawhide thong on the pony's head. During the day, he told himself, he was a Christian and a cowboy. But early morning, the time for himself, he was true to the spirits.

The body had been crudely buried under yellowed leaves and dirt, with a branch torn from a nearby juniper thrown over the head. It was the raw wound of the tree that caught Peter Charley's eye. It could be the mark of a bear, or a mountain lion come down close to the herd. But town was too near, too threatening to these dying predators.

He allowed the black to stand quietly. Horse and rider were close in to town, where the white men would soon rise and grumble, complain and scratch themselves and not see what waited for them. Peter Charley kneed the black pony sideways. There was a purpose to his early ride, there were old prayers buried in him he wished to renew. There was a friend lying blinded, there was a prayer to be offered that would ask for new light.

But the wounded juniper and the two buzzards circling overhead drove him to slide off the black pony and step near the torn juniper. He smelled the death before he found it. The woman's skirt, legs thick and white, the naked torso. Peter Charley had no emotion as he covered the white woman with his blanket. He knew her name and had received no recognition from her. That was not her wrong, that was the wrong of her kind. Now the woman was dead, nothing more than that.

Common sense told him not to go into Cimarron with the news but to return to Martin Smith and his calm authority. It did no good to have an Indian find the body of a white woman who was naked. He would let Martin Smith finish what had begun with the wounded juniper and the raucous, jeering birds.

The black pony bucked and lunged at the urgency of its rider. In two strides the little horse was in full run, headed back toward the Broken S.

He slept into the morning, exhausted and spent from the previous night. The feel of the woman was still in his hands

147

and belly as he gradually came awake. A commotion outside his window annoyed him, bothering the first decent sleep he had enjoyed in a long time.

He could not remember what had happened at first, only that he was no longer worried about much. Then he tasted his rotten mouth and saw the skinned places on his hands and remembered all in one convulsive second. Panic told him to run, but he forced himself to lie flat on the bed, as if a watcher was there outside the window, a spy near the door. Neighbors knowing what he had done.

As the pictures and the feelings came clearer, Buckminster calmed. She was nothing; no one would care. He belched and groaned, rolled over, and went to sleep.

SEVENTEEN

DEATH WAS A common matter in Cimarron. Drownings were not unusual when the river flooded or a wash ran high. A mangled ranch hand under a stampede was a sorry sight, a running horse, a leg in a dog-town hole, a broken neck for horse and rider. The ladies, too, were near death, from pneumonia and overwork, too many children too soon. Some even went mad, running into the grasslands screaming, scaring their families half to death.

Children's lives were more fragile; childbirth killed many mothers and infants. Fevers filled the new cemeteries with tiny graves, pox and chills, even snakes took their toll. And fights killed a fair number, fists, iron bars, knives, and pistols. The St. James Hotel bore more than its share of scars in the ceiling, evidence of hot tempers and poor aim.

But murder, and of a woman—that was unconscionable.

Blue heard the talk outside his window. It was early, and no one had come yet to his room. He rubbed his eyes and blinked, and there was more light, more shape and shadow. He was cautious getting out of the narrow bed, still dizzy and aching, but he needed to relieve himself.

Diaz had brought a light meal to him last night, and they had barely talked but enough to know that Mrs. Miller had not yet come back to the hotel. Blue wondered where she was. Then her name was spoken outside the open window and in the hallway, where he could hear a man walk, another man stop to talk. The words were spoken softly as if to keep them hushed, away from listening ears.

Blue grabbed for the edge of the bed, and the door opened. It was the kid, Diaz. He could see the shape well enough to know before the kid spoke up. The voice quavered. "Señor, I have come to help. It is needed, no?"

The voices outside rose in volume, and Blue caught bits of the words. "Dirt all over . . . damned Indian. Smith says . . . you can't trust them Indians. Smith . . . dead, by God." The voices passed and Blue turned his whole body toward where he knew Diaz was. "You tell me, I can hear them. You tell me what's wrong." He stood up slowly.

The kid was quiet, but a shift in his posture, a different sound told Blue he was crying. "It's Mrs. Miller, ain't it, Diaz?" He was guessing. "She didn't come back last night. Now they talking about the Indian. What happened?"

The sobbing told him he was right. He was suddenly dizzy and grabbed for the bed, sat down hard. Voices in the hall, outside the window, all speaking the same words, sounding the same alarm. He thought then about Peter Charley.

"They ain't blaming Peter Charley. He couldn't have done it. Not him." Blue reached up and caught the kid's arm, pulled hard on it.

The kid jumped back, and Blue couldn't hold him. "Señor, you can see. You are not blind."

The words tasted bitter to Blue. "Diaz, I ain't wanting folks to know that. Just a bit, don't want a fuss. Too much going on now anyway. You tell me what happened."

It was as if the kid recognized then that they were two drifters from the world around them, intruders in an ordered world suddenly gone wrong. Diaz was young but no innocent, no matter how he tried to play the part. And Blue was nothing more than a half-wild bronc tamer, blinded by chance and caught up in the storm around them.

"You help me to the backhouse, Diaz, and you tell me what the hell's going on."

Diaz tugged on the arm of this new Blue Mitchell, who

saw him and looked to him for help. Together they made the long passage to the backhouse. They could hear the confusion of the town, and when Mitchell asked if Diaz could tell who was talking, who gathered in the crowd near the hotel, Diaz knew the limits of the man's sight, and the limits of his own abilities.

"Señor, I do not know these people. There are ranchers, but not your Mr. Smith and his daughter. There are no women. There are miners, this I know from their black clothes, and drifters. Hard men, who talk quiet. I do not understand what they say, for they speak too fast. I do not understand the words, but I am afraid."

Diaz surprised himself with the confession, and as he spoke the damning words he looked cautiously at Blue Mitchell. There was no pity there, no sneering. Then Mitchell spoke, and Diaz listened, for the voice was sad and heavy with knowing. "Most folks, they know about death. But they panic 'round murder. Ladies like Mrs. Miller, we can't live without 'em, Diaz. They our saviors, kid. We're the sinners and the weak ones, women like her, they just know, they hold us and care for us. We can't live without 'em."

Diaz could not stop the tears, and they surprised him. He had not cried for his mother; he had not cried since he was a baby. Then he saw the shine in Blue Mitchell's eyes, and he knew that the señor felt the same terrible sadness.

When he spoke, the words were more for himself than any listening, but Diaz was there and he, too, felt the same thoughts. So he listened, and understood. "She was a good woman, and I never thanked her. It ain't much, speaking a few words of kindness. Thanking someone doing for you. But I never had the sense to speak my mind." Then the man stopped and Diaz felt him sag, saw the blank eyes squeeze shut.

"I ain't had the sense or kindness to say my thanks. Now it won't be said. God help me, I ain't much of a man."

His gut rumbled and woke him. Buckminster got up slowly. He was pure hungry, as he'd ever been even back gutting out a buffalo and chewing on the gall. There was times before the kill when no food got into a man's belly 'cepting cold water and old jerky.

He'd had his kill; now he was pure hungry. Buckminster flexed his large hands and watched the scabbed knuckles bend and crack. By God, that had been a woman, well suited to a man's appetites.

He hadn't been here before, not in a long time, maybe not ever. Pulled loose from what he knew, and complete. Full in his groin, strong again, back to a beginning where meat was took by the strongest, where hides had more value than human life. He'd been there once, deep in his memory. The smell on his hands tasted of blood.

A fancy buggy and a fine team, a mine, men who talked with him on the street. Meals in the hotel, foods he could not pronounce, tastes he'd never known. A fool's world, a false trap waiting for hard cash and small brains. A world he could break in half by his own raw strength.

Buckminster paced the floor, oblivious to the stink inside and the clamor of voices outside. He wanted more of whatever came to him, whatever fitted in his hands. Then he remembered the dead roan mare and his forgotten gear and he laughed, loud enough that two men on the street below looked around for the raucous noise.

A dead mare, a dead mine, a dead woman. By God, Albert Buckminster may be dead, but he went at it head first, and no man could deny him that.

He wanted food, but he had no cash. He knew he could walk into the hotel and take what he wanted, but that would be the end, not the beginning. Names went through his mind, past misdeeds, wrongs done to him. Men who used him, took from him, laughed with the riches from their greed.

The dead roan owed a bill at the livery; Longacre cost too much. It was Buckminster's deal now.

He stepped out into the bright sun and squinted hard, shielded his face and paid no attention to the clusters of men scattered on the streets. He knew what he wanted and where it waited for him.

The mattress poked into his backbone, and he sat up. He'd gone back to sleep, a restless, sweaty sleep, and when he woke, it was to the quick remembrance that Mrs. Miller was dead. Murdered. Blue's hands went to his head, and he gingerly rubbed the healed wound. She was dead.

Death wasn't a specter, not through his way of life. Like most of his kind, dying was only the end, not unexpected, not unwelcome. But this was a woman killed. Strangled, Doc Farmer had said when he came up to see Blue. Martin Smith had been with him, but the two men told him no more than that.

And he couldn't do nothing about it, trapped in a dusty room with drawn shades and no eyes. Blue shuddered, hauled himself up, and walked straight to the window. He could see its shape now, make out the light even behind the heavy material. He grabbed the draperies and felt their weight, smelled their musty, tired odor. He pushed handfuls aside and let in the full strength of the sun.

He gasped, let go of the material, covered his eyes, and waited until the throbbing slowed down. Like he'd been cracked on the head all over again. He turned away from the window, gradually opened one eye, then the other. Light could be seen, shapes of the bed and small table, even a hint of the patterned flowers on the wall. No color past light and dark, but the beginnings of lines and forms.

He glanced sideways at the window, and the pain bit him. He covered his eyes quickly, that light was too much. Then the shock of that brightness tired him, and he skidded on the floor as he went back to the bed. Too much and too soon, and instinct told him he would do more damage if this time he went at his usual pace.

He lay across the bed, bare feet trailing on the floor. His heart still pounded, and his lungs still worked. He could see, damn it, he could see and it would get better. If he could wait.

He rolled over and thought unwillingly of Mrs. Miller. His nightshirt bunched up around his belly, and he felt cold air tease his legs and groin. She would have covered him, her big hands surprising in their delicacy. She would have looked away as she rearranged him, tucked him in the covers, and left him sleeping. She would never know he could begin to see.

He was full-grown and healthy, his hands opened and closed with power in their scarred fingers, strength in their sinew and bone. Hands much like his murdered a woman. Hands like his but not his.

Blue was helpless with the feelings, addled like a babe messed his britches. A man walked free, and Blue could not go look for him, find him, accuse him, and offer final justice.

He let his head burrow in the pillow, and in only a few minutes he was asleep.

Flora was slightly disgusted with herself. She had not been able to speak freely, as she had intended to. She had planned to bring up her idea and let him think of it. She had panicked, faced with his actual presence, and she had not said what she had practiced and memorized.

So now she sat on the top rail of the fence and watched the horses. And knew that the moment was past her. The town exploded with the news about Mrs. Miller. It was no time to bring Blue Mitchell into the conversation. No time to suggest that he become her husband.

Husband—she tasted the word and enjoyed it. The idea had come to her on the trip into town late yesterday. Husband. She would present the fact to her father, and he would accept it.

Now her cowardice had lost her the moment, and she once more had to be patient and wait. The picture of Mrs. Miller covered with dirt and left in the brush was distressing. The whole town was talking; even the hands came in for a meal looking like they'd been struck by summer lightning.

These men were used to death. Why were they so affected? And of course her papa would not say more than the woman was found dead. Flora watched from her perch and settled in on the Indian, Peter Charley. Even though she recognized

154

he did not like her, there had been a moment, when Blue was first struck down, that she had felt comfortable with the strange man.

Something was different in the Indian, something secretive and dark. The thought shocked her that perhaps he might have killed the woman, then she corrected herself. If an Indian had killed a white woman, he would not stay around, unless he was hanging from a strong tree.

Peter Charley crossed the yard and came near where Flora sat high on her rail. As if the Indian knew she was thinking about him. He talked to himself, yet she knew she was meant to hear every word. The sheriff of Cimarron was asking anyone if they'd seen a traveler on the road. There were marks, signs of a struggle. Footprints that were blurred and unreadable. Flora realized the truth—Mrs. Miller was murdered. A killer was loose.

Peter Charley didn't give her time for hysterics, he continued his monotone about the activities. Mrs. Miller was in the back room of the barbershop. Laid out on a plank table, covered with yards of linen. No one sat with her; no one joined in absolution for her death. As an unwanted widow, the woman now lay in her death as lonely as in life.

All this information came in strange, sly observances from the Indian. Flora heard the words and climbed down from her perch, and the bright blue cloth of her skirt caught on a splinter. She stood on the ground, but the skirt was pulled above her knees.

Peter Charley was no longer nearby. Flora cursed both the Indian and the stubborn calico. First she talked under her breath as she tried to free herself, as befitting her station in life. Then she said "damn" out loud, and the heavens did not open up; she spit into the dirt and said "goddamn" this time while the material hung on the rail and no heads turned in disapproval, no eyes widened, no mouths dropped open from shock.

The skirt tore, and Flora ran to the house trailing unraveling cloth. Last night she had not been able to tell Blue how she felt about him, last night again she played out a role, one left by her deceased mother and enforced by her righteous father. She had been a participant in the one-act play but had delivered her true thoughts only in her mind.

It was again her turn; Mrs. Miller lay on a cold slab, her face distorted by a linen shroud. Flora Smith was free, young, alive.

Longacre had been a small matter easily remedied. The man made little sound as Buckminster choked him to death. There had been five bits in the front pocket and a coin worn as a lucky charm. And after a ten-minute search Buckminster found a tin box under a rat-piled bed. The box contained thirty dollars or more in stained, oily bills and a few coins.

And there was a stack of useless Confederate bills at the bottom of the box. Buckminster laughed—the old fool. Longacre was a Southerner too shamed to be proud. Never said nothing out loud, never talked politics or ideals. And look what it got him. The bills were neatly stacked, a monument to a stupid cause. A memory of a man's life. So now the old man was dead and his folly exposed. Buckminster laid the fool out on the smelly bed and scattered Confederate bills on the pitiful chest. Enough of a formal burial for a Southerner.

Now there was money in his pockets, and the hunger came back full force. By God, he was starving, and thirsty. No more of that whiskey from the saloon's back door. Only Lambert's finest. And as Buckminster patted the store of money, he knew this time he didn't have to crawl 'round the back and bribe that fool kid into stealing. No, this time he could walk in the front door and order what he pleased and know that the dead Southerner, Longacre, paid the bill.

And there weren't nothing could be done about it.

He was respectable now, like the bankers and ranchers and the lawyers come to town, drive their rigs up to the front and that breed kid takes 'em over to the livery, stores them until they's needed again.

Can't do that no more; old Longacre, he ain't feeling too well.

Buckminster was careful going out the livery stable door and timed his exit so no one watched. He aimed toward the fine hotel, and when he got there, he stared at the front steps. Stone they were, worn stone with an iron railing going from top to bottom. Pretty, the big man thought, a touch of Lambert's fancy French mind. No good to hold up a man or a bronc tied there waiting, but still real pretty.

It was dark inside even with the long window built from the floor to the tin ceiling. A waste, Buckminster thought. Pure extravagance; too easy to get shot through, thief could break in and steal a man's hair while he weren't looking.

He shook his head. The world was tamed now, and the men in their suits drove fancy buggies, rode high-stepping horses. These were the ones stealing from a man now, not the Indians and the breeds, the outlaws and rustlers.

Hell, a man couldn't see what robbed him blind anymore. It was more than Buckminster understood.

A small girl approached him, wearing a black skirt and a lacy notion 'round her narrow waist. She said that he wasn't allowed in the hotel dining room, but he grinned and pushed past her, and she stepped back with her hand to her mouth. Buckminster liked the recognition.

There was a wide doorway, and he knew the sounds coming from it; china and metal and glasses all making noise. With voices that rose over the muted sound and argued, questioned, talked loud about important matters.

Buckminster walked in the dining room of the St. James Hotel and seated himself at the biggest table he could find. It was set for six; he spread out his elbows on the white linen and planned to use every one of the utensils surrounding him. It pleased him, 'cause a man needed only a knife to eat a meal and a tin cup or the bottom of his hand to drink cold water. But this is what folks paid for, and by God, he was going to get his money's worth.

EIGHTEEN

As CIMARRON'S ELECTED law, Roland Bellson agreed he would ride out again to the site, soon. Right now he sat with the men who got him elected, and tried to work up the energy. Past fifty, looking too close at sixty, Bellson had seen the worst in mankind, and a killing was no surprise. But murder, of a woman—he hadn't counted on that kind of death.

He'd been tough, and good at his job for years. Now he was only tired. He sat and listened, waiting for inspiration.

He sat next to Grant Forman, who claimed twenty thousand acres running the edge of the Ponil River. The runt, Homer Nelson, sat puffed up like a child and let his booted feet dangle over the chair as if he didn't care. Joe Morris, part of the group even though he ran the Silver Eye over across the street, sat quiet, as if he knew he was included on sufferance.

Martin Smith was the fifth man. His face was thinned down, his hair mussed, his eyes watery and reddened. He was tired, as all the men in the circle were tired, worn with the worry about the murder. Worried about their own families and the town, the outlying ranches. Worried that their safe little world was fast going to Hell.

Albert Buckminster made no impression on these men; their thoughts were centered on solving the problem. Morris looked up and barely caught the big man's eye and nodded, but that was all the greeting Buckminster received.

Bellson tried to back out of riding again. "I ain't keen on leaving town again, you don't mind. Chances are the son who, ah . . . did in Mrs. Miller is walking the streets here or long gone, a drifter mistook his quarry. Mrs. Miller, now she weren't much of a looker, but she was a woman. Women can drive some men to, ah . . . killing again."

Bellson stared at the surface of the table. Come time for a fancy meal, that smooth table'd be covered in a white cloth and spread with silver, glass, and flowered plates. Lambert kept his standards, never mind he was living next to the end of the world. Been a private cook for presidents, it was said, lived in that country, ah . . . France. Nice table, Bellson thought. The tips of his fingers touched the glossy surface. No fool yet carved their name there. Sign of Lambert's power.

Martin Smith stretched his hand across the table. "Rolly, sheriff." That was all the man could say, which was unusual. Smith tried again, and Roland Bellson listened. "Rolly, you're most likely right. The killer's either gotten out of here fast or is right here in town. But, you know, there are things . . ." Here Smith got stuck again, and Bellson got worried, cautioned himself for patience. Martin Smith had a level head, thought clear, never got rattled. Whatever had the man now, it still was worth waiting for him to speak. "Rolly, you know what to look for. Bits of cloth, footprints. Hellfire, the man had to walk around there some. There has to be more than just a body. The son of a . . . the killer had to be waiting, or get there somehow. You go look, you'll see."

Bellson had gone over these very points in his mind endlessly, but he had to convince Martin Smith of the logic of his thoughts. "Martin, that-there clearing got trampled over when your Indian, that Peter Charley, turned in the news. Now he said, that Indian said there was a dead horse a mile or so downriver. Broke neck, so Peter Charley claims, and I believe that Indian, never mind he's a buck Christian. But . . ."

Bellson saw one of the footprints, off to a corner, a big

print of a big man. And the dead horse was a roan mare; might be the one belonging to Buckminster at the other table.

Some of his thinking must have passed to Smith, for the old man looked hard at Buckminster, and Bellson turned in his seat and watched the big man. The temper was there, and the size. And if it was his mare, that put him in the right place. Buckminster grinned when he became aware of their scrutiny and lifted his knife in a crude salute.

Hellfire, Bellson thought. He's a-sitting there eating like nothing's wrong and he's hungry. That's all, hungry. No killer done what was done to that woman would come sit in a fancy place and eat in full sight of the law.

Bellson was conscious of Martin Smith's tension. "I'll talk to him, Martin. But he's already told his story to Longacre, over to the livery. Went, ah . . . over to places in town this morning, when the news come in. Longacre, he said that Buckminster showed up mussed and tired last night, cursing a dead horse. Said your daughter passed him on the road, wouldn't give him a ride. Said too he saw Mrs. Miller, said good evening to her. Wondered what she was doing that far from town. Don't sound much like a killer, talking all that to Longacre, cursing his horse." Smith only looked at him, and Bellson got nervous. "I'll try again, Martin. Soon as I come, ah . . . back from that place. Ride out now, talk to Buckminster later, when he's done eating. That suit you?" He couldn't help the bite of anger in his question, as if Martin Smith doubted his ability to function on his own. Been ranching for years, taking care of a wife and six children. He could do what needed doing. No help from Martin Smith.

Smith said nothing, only stared. Bellson got uncomfortable. "Hell, Martin, I just don't know."

Bellson left the table and passed close enough to Buckminster that he could smell the man. Buckminster lived near Cimarron for fifteen years now; hard to think of him as a murder suspect. Worked hard, the big man did. Might not make the best choices, but he paid his bills most times and kept out of trouble. No one cared much for the man, hard to get along with. But a killer—Bellson couldn't put the picture together.

It had to be a drifter. No one Bellson knew could kill a woman like Mrs. Miller with his bare hands. He shied away from the rest of what happened to the woman, what Dr. Farmer talked about as he examined the body. No one Bellson knew could do such a thing.

The sheriff stood on the hotel step, scratched under the edge of his hat, and watched the town. There were few women walking along the streets, maybe three children almost grown. The town was spooked, primed, plain downright scared.

The law was spooked, too, Bellson admitted, but only to himself. Not like a gunfighter or a bank robber. A cautious man could handle these types, but not what had happened to the woman. Bellson sighed and looked to the right at a wagon drawn by an unmatched team. The driver carried a rifle across his lap. When the sheriff looked left, two men crossed the street and did not speak. Bellson could guess the question in each man's mind, feel the tension in their stiff-legged walk.

He finally climbed on the patient bay tied to the rail and reined the horse east, out of town, along the wide dirt track that eventually led to Denver and beyond to the grasslands. He was going a short distance, to the site of the murder.

Homer Nelson kicked at the air and rubbed his nose, grunting in anger. "By God, if Rolly finds the son, I'll kill him with my own hands. No man treats a decent woman that way, or any woman. We got us a rogue."

Despite his diminutive size there was no folly in Nelson's statement. In the talk of mountain men, Nelson was pure quill, with the heart of a lion and the grit and guts to fight ten times his own weight and never quit, never give in.

Martin Smith straightened in the hard chair. Grant Forman uttered what would be an agreement to Nelson's flat statement. And Joe Morris said he'd like another drink of the good whiskey. Maybe the breed kid would get some. None of these men thought about or saw their company in the din-

161

ing room. They were turned inward, experiencing a revival of habits and patterns once put aside in the wake of civilized times.

Buckminster sat in a neighborly frame of mind and ate his meal. Beefsteak and fried potatoes and lots of both, none of the fancy food offered by the Frenchie menu. He rubbed a torn loaf of bread in the juice and gnawed on the soggy crust. Tasted good to him, and he licked as the juice ran down his chin. By God, it was good the Frenchie was out of town. A man could set in the fancy dining room and eat what he wanted an' no fool Frenchie talking odd and telling a body what to do.

Buckminster belched loudly, and still his neighbors paid him no mind. It was only fitting a man ate well when he was down on his luck and then came into good fortune. A sign, by God, a message the rest of these damned fools still needed to learn.

The room was quiet. The four men in the corner barely noticed when Buckminster paid out his generous five dollars in bills and shoved the chair hard enough to tip it over when he left the table.

The kid came up once, around noon, with food, and told Blue his clothes were in a closet down the hall. The kid's face was drawn and he was quiet, barely speaking even when asked a direct question. But Diaz helped Blue down the hall, and when Blue kept his hand on the kid's shoulder and said something about Mrs. Miller, the kid shrugged as if it didn't matter. Blue knew better but said nothing more.

He bumped back into the room, and found where Diaz had left the clothes and the tray of food. He knew he still couldn't depend on his eyes, especially after he found himself at the end of the hall, having missed his own door. His head ached again, as it did when he tried to see, so he let his fingers discover what was served for a meal and came up with beans, something that smelled like cooked apples, and a tortilla filled with spiced meat. Blue was hungry again and didn't need a fork and knife, or eyes, to fill his belly with this food.

He slept immediately after eating and woke in a sweat, his heart pounding. An enemy waited outside the door, where Blue couldn't see his shape and color. He forced himself to lie still and fight through the effects of a dream, listen to daylight reason.

There was no one near the door; Blue half laughed, got up, and then cursed as he bumped into the wall again. He found the clothes where Diaz had put them, piled on a chair. Habit made getting dressed possible, except for buttoning the shirt on straight. He couldn't focus to find the holes, and his fingers were thick and clumsy. He was back to frustration and rising temper, fighting to stay calm. Trying to outguess his boots made it all worse, and Blue sat down and shook his head at himself. After three attempts to pull the damned things on, he threw one across the room and was immediately contrite when he heard glass break.

Then tiredness swept over him, quickly, without a hint, taking him by surprise. He didn't think putting on clothes qualified as hard work, yet here he was, head nodding, eyes burned shut, sleepy, needing to lie down. He rested his hands on his thighs and felt the leg muscles tremble; all of him shook, and when he opened his eyes, there was no light, no shape. Nothing. Blind again.

Hell. He gave up and lay back on the bed, careful to keep his feet on the floor. One foot had a boot on it, weren't proper to lie in bed with your boots on and too much work to take the damned things off. Blue laughed at himself then, 'cause someone had to laugh at the fool. The laughter turned to a sorry cry, and he knew he had lost a friend. Damn a man who would hurt a woman, damn him to Hell.

Time left him again. He slept for more than an hour, and when he woke, it was to a new dream, a new enemy stirring outside the door. He came out of the bed fast, grabbed for the bedpost, reaching for a nonexistent pistol hanging there. He stopped hard, shuddered, aware of his useless being. Naked, defenseless; he hated what he was right then.

163

It was footsteps, most likely Diaz. Come back with more food, a need to talk. About the murder, about most anything. Blue was restless and bored, hot-tempered like a confined horse.

The dream came roaring over him again as he stood holding on to the bedpost. The chestnut colt reared out of his memory, the scene sharp and clear as if the colt was in the room. Hooves above his head, eyes white-rimmed, teeth drawn back over bloodless lips. Blue crouched, his arms raised from the punishment pounding inside his head. He cried out, knowing it was a dream yet helpless with the image before him.

And it was the girl who cried at his odd actions and spoke his name out loud, over and over, calling him. Tearing the chestnut colt out of Blue's mind and banishing him from the small hotel room.

Blue sat on the bed, rubbing his eyes furiously. His face was hot. He knew he had been the fool. "Miss, what . . . ?" She got started ahead of him, and Blue shut his mouth and listened. Her tone was normal, and he thanked her for that sense of delicacy. "Why, Mr. Mitchell, you're dressed. And you did fine, although you should see what you've done with your shirt." Here he could tell she was flustered by her own words, and he wanted to comfort her.

She stood only a few feet distant from him. If he half opened his eyes, the strong light from the broken window did not bother him. She wore pants; he could see that much easily. Her form was outlined by the confining garment, and Blue rejoiced that his sight had come back to give him the treat. Her face glowed, and her hair was blown loose from its pins and touched her face and neck. He stood up without thinking and put a finger to the edge of her neck, where a long curl swept the collar of her man's shirt. He sighed the joy of seeing and touching a lovely young woman.

"Blue, can you see? Really see? Oh." He closed his eyes again. As if she understood, Flora gently began to rebutton his shirt front correctly. And when her fingers, by accident, brushed his chest, Blue quickly opened his eyes.

"But that Mrs. Miller, she said . . ." They were both chastened by the sound of the dead woman's name.

"Dr. Farmer told Papa you would never see. That's what he told Papa. From that terrible blow to your head. Papa shot the colt, you know. Before he even knew whether you would live or die. Peter Charley dragged the body away for the coyotes to eat. Daddy . . . Papa didn't want me to know all this, but I saw the tracks and heard the coyotes. I knew."

She went off in a direction Blue couldn't follow, so he sat back down and prepared himself to wait and figure. He sure didn't understand women.

"Last night, oh, dear. Blue, Mr. Mitchell, last night I came here and acted . . . let me explain. Papa, I think, wants us to marry. That way you will be taken care of because he knew the stallion was bad and didn't tell you, and I will be at home with him always. He's old now and scared, and I think he wants . . ."

In quick succession Flora's hand brushed Blue's stomach above the waist of his jeans, and he jumped from the contact as she put together some more words out of her mind and got herself angry in the process. Blue sat gasping, holding on for dear life against the ride the girl was giving him. She was a talker and knew her mind; he'd give her that much and more.

"You deceived me last night." She poked him in the chest and then shoved him. "You made me think you were a cripple, that you were helpless. You let me make a fool . . . say all kinds of . . . you're hateful."

She shoved him again, and he grabbed the two hands, capturing them between his own. He stared hard and could even see the contrast of her fine hands and his big, clumsy ones, stained and cracked still from their lifetime of work. He was inclined to agree with the girl about her estimation of him, but he also had to grin at her unbounded fury, and the grin got her madder at him. She stamped a foot, and he laughed out loud, pleased with the whole performance.

Her hands slipped from his, and Blue ducked, fearing the

worst, but she caught him again by laughing. She was a wonder, Miss Flora Smith.

She would sit next to him on the bed, but he gestured toward the window, where Mrs. Miller sat and watched over him while he was an invalid. The girl paid him no mind. "Blue, dear Blue. It's a little late for modesty. And besides, I would bet the window's glare would hurt your eyes. And look, there's broken glass everywhere, where someone threw a boot and broke the window." He could really hear the grin this time, and he grinned back at her. "Besides, Blue, I've seen you in your nightshirt, and you might as well be naked in that thing. And I just buttoned your shirt, so don't be silly."

A serious note came into her voice. "They're downstairs, talking and not doing anything. Except for Sheriff Bellson, who Papa says is really useless. He rode out a while back. I guess he went . . . but there's no one upstairs, no one to see us."

Then her voice changed again, and Blue wanted to protect her, take her in his arms and hold her. "Blue, I'm afraid. Really afraid, and I don't want to be. Papa is so old, and this is all so terrible. Blue."

He allowed the girl to sit back beside him, and instinct brought the two of them closer, until it was only natural that she rested her head on his shoulder and his arm moved to support her, and she was finally allowed to feel safe.

NINETEEN

Buckminster decided to walk around the inside of the hotel and see for himself. He walked the grand tour, strolled through the parlor, snorting in amusement at the velvet draperies and patterned carpet, the fancy laces and clouded glass. A tall clock ticked endlessly in a fine-grained case, and the air smelled of dried flowers. Most of it was wasted on Buckminster's sensibilities.

He went through double-swinging doors down a hallway. Doors on each side, more rooms for fools to stay in. Beds with ruffles and flutters around them, beds for fools. Buckminster scratched an armpit, sniffed, and thought he might need a bath.

He opened a door and startled a couple. The man's hand was up under the woman's skirt, and her breasts were exposed. The couple pulled apart, and Buckminster grinned at them and closed the door. He knew them; the man had five kids, the woman was a maid to the hotel. Fools, more fools.

He didn't think much on the morals of the married man and the rough-faced whore from the kitchen, but the sight of them got him thinking, remembering. Tasting the flesh of that ugly old woman out on the road. He absently rubbed the swelling on the top of his head and thought of the fight she'd put up, the pleasure he'd taken. She'd been better than old Longacre, more fun when she fought and harder to kill. Longacre had been only cash; the woman was raw pleasure.

Stairs turned a corner and disappeared. Buckminster put his foot on the bottom step, and it made no noise. He liked the heavy carpet, the way it gave under his foot and kept silent. It eased a man's steps, made him feel rich.

The full measure of his considerable weight came down on each tread, and his big hand slid on the mahogany railing as he went upstairs. There was no sound but his breathing, no noise but his heartbeat, and no feeling but the swollen pulse in his groin and the sweetness of his memories.

Diaz smelled the ugly man. Rank sweat and more that Diaz could not name. He trusted his instincts; he was frightened all over again. Before this ugly man had gone up the stairs, a woman had been here. To see the sick one, Blue Mitchell. Diaz thought she was still in that room.

The other smell Diaz recognized was fear. His own fear.

Peter Charley saw the truth, but it was a truth different from what the white man saw. The Indian patiently sat on his heels in the brush and waited for the white man with the star pinned to his chest to see what was in front of him. The man spent too long walking endlessly around the shallow grave where the woman had lain. Kneeling, grabbing for dirt and letting it slip through his spread fingers as if a miracle would appear there in front of him.

The truth that Peter Charley saw was past this place, down the road where a horse had been tangled in brush and forced to let a man catch it. The truth was the corpse of that horse, eyes rolled back in the torn skull, teeth bared in final defiance. The prints were there, all around the dead horse. Boots that were patched twice on the outside of the left boot, boots with a nail head gouging out holes from the right heel. Simple to read, waiting only for the eyes to see and know the truth.

The same hands that had shamed the woman had killed the horse. Peter Charley saw that truth and could not understand why the white man with the star that spoke of his power could not see what was in front of him.

There was some sympathy in him. Earlier too many of the fools had walked in horror around the corpse and wiped out some of the enemy's mark. Peter Charley watched and said nothing. For they saw only his Indian color and his Christian name and knew he worked for another man and did not listen to him.

The decision was for Peter Charley to make, now that he saw the best the white man could do and it angered him. The big one who made the prints still walked in town, a man slipped free of his own laws, loose now from his people's rules. The girl was in town again. Martin Smith's girl, who had eyes for the blinded horse tamer.

Peter Charley knew she would be with the horse tamer, and he knew that the big man would soon find her, find her blind protector. In that girl's mind was the intent to marry Blue Mitchell; Peter Charley heard the words spoken by the father. They made no sense, the two of them, father and child, yet they had in their hearts this mistake they would each make.

The girl had gone to the hotel. She did not know of the complete killing of Mrs. Miller, as did few women of the town. These things were not seemly for white women to know. For white women to hear.

And what was not known, the truth that was not spoken, could kill another woman, a child. The truth was what Peter Charley knew, and he must now choose what next to do.

Then the white man with the star climbed on his tired bay horse and rode off, and Peter Charley sat for a while, watching, thinking. Away from the white man's unseeing eyes. Finally he climbed on the black pony and walked him cautiously along the riverbank, close to the dead mare. He had to make a choice.

It was the fat man. That smell—it was his only. The fat man had been seated in the fine dining room and had been served by a frightened girl, and now he was gone. But Diaz thought the man was in the hotel. He could imagine the sound of those feet, and he cringed from the expected blow.

169

It was the cook yelling at him for more vegetables, more potatoes, a fresh haunch of beef. Get going, stupid boy, do your job. The cook, not the fat man with the ugly temper and the bad smell.

There were pots he must still scrub and more of the vegetables to scrape off, and the pretty little girl who liked to tease him. But the smell haunted Diaz, troubling him deeply. He fussed with a knife, picked it up, and ran his thumb along the blade, putting it down only when the cook yelled at him. He thought to do his work, but the instinct picked at him until he turned around and around in a dizzying circle, and the cook laughed while he was cursing Diaz. It was not right, it did not taste good. But Diaz did not know what to do.

The girl had gone upstairs to the horse tamer. Diaz had heard her. The fat man's smell still hung in the air. Those thoughts twisted inside Diaz until it was all he could do to remain in the kitchen.

Roland Bellson allowed that his bay was tired and so was he. His own bones ached from the useless ride and the time spent poking at mussed-up ground, staring into unseen distances, and making guesses he could not prove. The bay carried him slowly back to Cimarron and swerved by habit toward the livery stable. It was as good an idea as any; Bellson felt he had no more need for the horse right now.

Besides, he was hungry again, even though it'd been two hours or less since he ate over at the hotel.

The inside of the stable was dark and closed, no door open to the back, no horses dozing in the pens. The aisle was littered with damp straw and old manure, and there were bridles tangled on the floor, a saddle in a heap near the back door. Longacre was slipping, Bellson thought. The man was an argumentative son of a bitch, but he usually kept the stable clean and picked up, most times.

Bellson recognized the saddle as belonging to Martin Smith. The man had come in early and hadn't left yet. Most likely, Bellson thought as he walked his bay the length of the stable, Martin was still at the St. James, talking and thinking and getting nowhere as fast as he was, or faster.

He expelled a great gust of air; it stank in here of ammonia, dust, and spoiled feed. But it weren't fair of him to condemn a man, even old Longacre, for how he kept his own place. Where the hell was the man? By now he usually had his hand on the bay's bridle, fussing and clicking his tongue.

He got tired of the wait. "Longacre, by God, where are you? I got business to attend to, official business, if you want, you sorry old son. Come on, get out here and get this horse."

The high whinny of a lonesome sorrel tied in the corner answered Bellson. He didn't much like the silence, the lack of commotion, he didn't trust not hearing the querulous voice, a door slammed in disgust. He slapped the bay into a close stall, leaving it to chew on wisps of hay and not run off.

He opened the door to the tiny room Longacre called an office. Flies buzzed in a rising chorus, sunlight lazed through the filthy window and shaded its bold pattern on Longacre's blue face. The eyes bulged, covered with industrious flies. The hands turned up like useless claws, the mouth hung open, thick with the protruding tongue, and a dung beetle appeared through the broken teeth.

Bellson vomited; he couldn't help it. He went to his knees and vomited again. Zachery Longacre had been his friend.

Martin Smith was only half listening to Homer drone on about percentages and rising costs. He heard Bellson's voice, heard the fear in it, unusual for a man who once talked a man out of a killing while he himself carried no gun. Bellson was slowed by age, like himself, Smith mused, but he wasn't usually afraid.

The voice carried equal fear and misery, he decided. So he got up out of his chair, groaning with the effort, and left the room without excusing himself or explaining to Homer and the rest.

As he figured, Homer shut up and came with him, and Grant Forman. And Joe Morris, although Martin didn't see much use in the man. Bellson was planted outside the livery barn. He looked old, as old as Martin Smith felt. The man's face was dead white, and he kept wiping his mouth and spitting.

Smith got closer and could smell the fear, the stench of a body's loosened system. He had to avert his face and take a deep breath, and even then Bellson showed no embarrassment.

"Zach's dead, Martin. Murdered. Twisted his neck like he weren't no more effort than a cur dog. Big man did it, big hands broke Zach's neck. "Most yanked his head easy. Ugliest thing I seen in a long time. Hell, Zach, he had nothing worth taking. Kept his money to the bank, not worth much inside that barn, not worth the killing done to him."

Bellson seemed to take notice then of Martin Smith and others around him. The man's pride resurfaced, and he pulled himself back into being the law. "Martin, you do me a favor. You keep these folks out of the barn. Hell . . . I don't want folks gawking at him now. You keep 'em out. I'll get the doc. Get myself cleaned up." Then Bellson slipped back for a moment, staring into the damp eyes of his longtime friend. The fear came up again, and its appearance shook Martin Smith to his soul. "Martin, we got a monster loose here. We got more trouble'n I can handle. It's more . . . I'm scared. You can smell it on me, like a greenhorn plumb fresh from Kansas."

It was meant to be a joke, a poor one but a try at normalcy. And it didn't work. Martin Smith shook badly, and Roland Bellson's belly cramped on him again as he started down the street, looking for the doc and wanting to rub the picture out of his eyes.

Peter Charley allowed the black pony to drift down a side street. He tied the black near the side of the fancy hotel, where he was not allowed to trespass in the white man's world.

He stared up at the great blank windows and rubbed his

172

jaw. Voices rang out near the stable of the old man with the foul temper, but the hotel was quiet, stately.

Peter Charley broke the rules. He went in the door near the hot kitchen and followed a passageway toward the big front parlor. He started badly when a thin, black-haired child whose eyes were light and frightened stepped into the hallway in front of him.

The child's voice quavered, but the words were firm. "There is something wrong. Upstairs. She is there. And the fat man . . ."

They both heard the sound; Peter Charley pushed past the child and withdrew his knife. As he ran toward the stairs, he heard the child running behind him.

TWENTY

A STRAND OF hair tickled his nose and he wanted to pick it off, but his arms were full of a beautiful girl, and he couldn't quite let go. Not just then. So Blue worked the fine hair until it stuck in the side of his mouth, and he laughed silently at the foolishness of it all.

Flora sensed his laughter and lifted her head. Her eyes were close to him, so he could see their expression; she, too, was laughing. He watched her face and saw details, the lightest freckles, the thick lashes framing the eyes, the specks of color in the dark iris. He grinned, pleased that he could make out the slightest imperfection, and she moved away from him as if the grin had been an impertinence.

From that distance, about two feet, Blue could no longer see her clearly. His eyes blinked rapidly with the strain and his head ached, he recognized the familiar, dreary pattern. He'd strained the injury, and it would plague him now until he rested. But the new ache was worth the pleasure of seeing Flora Smith so close by.

The girl drew herself together and opened her mouth as if to speak. This time Blue got in ahead of her, anxious she not think badly of him. He had been far too intimate with her when she had been afraid. "Miss, thank you. I know you been trying to make it easier for me. Fear, well . . . I never knew being afraid like this before." He had to think out each word and get it right, for he wasn't making a joke or teasing;

he was attempting to say what he felt, and the chore was quickly getting away from him. "Fear don't belong to just ladies. This not seeing . . . ain't nothing like that fear. Makes a man helpless, less than he is. I . . . ain't no other way but to say thank you. For trying to help."

Before she got started, Blue put a hand over her mouth and could see the differences. Any blind fool could do that. Dirt ingrained in his knuckles, that damned scar 'cross his thumb; the mouth soft, the lips tender, the skin of the face so very fine. Fresh lovely eyes that burned in anger now, that softened as he continued to talk and gave him back a measure of his pride.

"Miss, whatever got to Mrs. Miller, I won't let it come to you. You can't ride out to your ranch alone now. We got to get you downstairs, with your daddy." The next was difficult, and his tongue got tied up from speaking. "Miss, you and your daddy, and that talk of marrying. He's a big man, your daddy. And I'm proud to ride for him. He don't owe nothing on that chestnut colt. I saw it right there, in those eyes. But I was bragging and showing off, knowing I could handle anything that colt could throw at me. Shows me how wrong I was. Ain't no more to it than that.

"There ain't no holding you to your talk, you and your daddy. But I thank you both. More'n you'll know. There ain't no need, you understand? Not that you ain't a prize, but there ain't no cause now. I'm proud of the asking, but I got a lot of my own to do yet, 'fore I could be part of a family."

It was more words than he'd strung together, but it was close to what he was feeling. Family and pride. And debts. All a man owned when his worldly goods were a horse and saddle was his pride and his honor.

He couldn't get Lela Miller from his mind, and hesitated. But the words needed to be said. "Miss, now you and your daddy most likely thought of this, but I want it said, too. Mrs. Miller, she took a lot from the folks around here and didn't let on how it hurt. And she took care of me when I was pure wild. You put up a stone for her, you make it the finest and you tell the world all about her heart and . . . ah, hell, miss. I can't say it, but you got to know what I mean.''

"Blue Mitchell, will you marry me?"

Blue touched the girl very carefully on the wrist, where her hand lay on the edge of his bed. "Miss, you ain't thinking again. But I thank you, and know what you're trying . . . I think . . . for Mrs. Miller. As if we could bring her back. Being killed like that, cold and mean, it ain't no way for a lady like she was to die.''

Flora stiffened as if Blue had proposed an indecency to her. He had done less than what they had shared only a few moments ago. It could only be what was just said . . . "killed like that, cold and mean.'' Maybe no one had told the girl how Mrs. Miller had died.

"Miss Flora, don't you know? Other than she's dead?"

She did not hear him. Blue squinted and strained his eyes and knew that she was watching something past the door. Her eyes grew wide and frightened, and her hand went to her mouth. She drew back from Blue's touch. He ducked out of instinct and came around, up from the bed and ready to fight.

A fist crashed on his shoulder, a fist carrying a knife. The blade cut through his shirt and drew a wide line down his forearm off his elbow, scraped across his hip. Blue kept moving, hit the floor, and kicked out backward at what had come at him.

Flora screamed and rolled off the bed, landing in the corner, where she curled up in self-protection. Her scream didn't stop while she crossed her arms over her face, as if such tender flesh could save her.

Blue's hip burned, and his arm was numb. He rolled fast, conscious only that he needed a weapon. He didn't know what he was fighting. The girl's scream unnerved him. He needed to wipe his eyes clear and get himself ready.

"You righteous son of a bitch.''

The words directed him. Blue looked to the right of the door, just inside the room. He could judge the size of the man. He could almost see the sharp edge of the knife in the big

176

hand. The voice wasn't familiar to Blue, yet its speech was curious, words from an older time.

"You got no business with that gal. You blind son, I'm here to take her, and you get yourself out'a my way or I'll take that pretty hair a your'n for a trinket."

Blue thought the man was pure crazy. The man threw back his head and laughed as if nothing could stop him. "That hair a your'n, that gold color'll sell to the Injuns. They like that gold; they pay more for a scalp the color a gold. Us white men, we pay out our souls for the metal while them dumb Injuns buy up a gold-colored scalp and count themselves rich. It plumb breaks us, that damn metal, and we pay for it."

Blue drew a leg up under him and quickly rubbed at his eyes. He couldn't make sense of the ramblings, but he was willing to let the big man go on.

Flora had stopped screaming; now she sobbed into her arms and choked, trying to wipe her runny nose and not make any sound. To keep that terrible man from staring at her. He was fascinated by Blue; she could not understand what he was saying all about scalps and gold, but he talked intently to Blue, and Flora shook while she huddled in the corner.

Then she wiggled under the bed. Her face was flat against the floor, and she could smell dust. Past the fringe covering the other side of the bed, she could see Blue's one stockinged foot, a big hole in the toe. She giggled and then sighed, comforted by the illusion of safety.

Blue couldn't see where the girl had gone, but he howled to distract the big man. The loud voice joined him, laughing until it drowned out Blue's words. "That gal, she thinks she's safe under the bed. Hiding like a baby child. Thinks she's safe, does she? I'll play with you a while and then she and I, we'll get right to my business. Or pleasure."

Blue came up off his knees then, knowing he was close to committing suicide, but he couldn't do nothing. He could not outguess what he could not see. His bare foot hit broken glass, and he staggered, lunging for the big shape that moved easily away from him. The loud voice taunted Blue; helpless, he swept his arms in a wide circle. He caught up the heavy water pitcher and slammed it against the wall. It broke with a strong sound, and Blue felt the edge of the raw glass. Now he had a weapon.

He could not judge. He could guess and try, but he could not see well enough to direct his next move. Blue lunged straight forward, aiming the broken pitcher toward the dark mound of the big man's belly.

Buckminster watched the attack, commended the blind cowboy for his guts, and laughed at his futile gesture. When the cowboy got too close, Buckminster would step to the side, and the blind eyes would throw the cowboy flat into the wall. Buckminster laughed and moved sideways.

Blue saw enough to turn with the big man and jab the glass edge at him. The weapon stuck hard, and Blue leaned into the effort, muscle giving way under his hand. Then he was picked up, shaken, and slammed into the wall. Blue kicked out, heard the gasp, and tasted the foul breath in his face. He smelled hot blood, but the big man held him in midair and laughed instead of doubling over in gutted agony, and two big hands wrapped around Blue's throat.

No light, no air; his heart raced and then slowed. Muscle and bone collapsed. Blue hung from Buckminster's hands and began to die slowly.

There was no fun in this. Buckminster dropped the body and watched the cowboy roll loose on the floor. Blood ran from the cut arm, the eyes were closed, the face turned gray, and even the mouth was blue. Buckminster kicked at the cowboy, and his thigh hurt. He looked down. By God, that blind son got him. The leg of his pants ran red, drops hitting the scuffed floor. Buckminster stared. Cut, by God. The blind horse tamer got him. He saw the heavy broken glass of the pitcher, sticky with blood, and laughed again, wiped his mouth and spit. Cut, by God, and with a fancy glass gewgaw from the hotel itself.

Absently he wiped his own knife on his pants. That stung

178

him, and he saw he'd been cleaning the knife in his own blood. Damn fool thing to do; so he changed hands and cleaned the blade on the other leg. It was important the knife be damned clean.

She could see the top of a head. She could touch it if she stretched out and pushed herself with her feet against the wall. It was easy to slide on the floor, but the dust tickled her nose. She could reach out and smooth the blond hair and even stroke the damp forehead if she pushed herself far enough along the wooden floor.

But she could also see the dark pants and the dirty boots. And there was blood pooling near one boot, until the boots moved and the blood was smeared. It was a disgrace to treat a wood floor in such a manner. Papa would be disgusted.

Flora put out a finger tentatively, expecting to be scolded. But there was no sound other than a methodical, rasping noise. She touched the shiny red surface, and the texture was smooth, warm. She put her finger in her mouth much as a child would do when first crawling, and sucked on the end, then withdrew the finger and looked at it.

The blood was sticky and sweet, not what she expected at all.

The head so close to her stirred, the blond hair shifted, and she watched as dust balls danced on the yellow strands. The head rolled over, and more dust twirled around in the air. It was fascinating, and Flora was quite startled when the head moved closer to her and she could see the eyes try to open and focus on her.

There was confusion in those remarkable eyes, which were familiar to her but she could not quite remember. The eyes found her, blinked twice, and then closed, as if in suffering. Flora did not know what was happening, but she did try to inch closer and push the blond hair back from the white forehead. Perhaps that was what was the matter.

"Flora, you all right . . . hurt?"

The mouth formed words and sounds, but she didn't comprehend their meaning. She smiled sweetly to reassure, and the eyes widened. Then a big hand came down, and the face and its lovely blond hair were dragged away from her view. Flora curled up in a ball again and wanted to cry.

He deliberately stared into the ugly face but could not really see. The breath flooded him, and the face contorted into a parody of concern when he flinched. The words were a mockery of his blindness, and still Blue did not respond. "Little boy, you all right? I surely didn't mean to hurt you even if you was the one stuck that-there glass in me. You blind pig, you stuck poor old Albert for no reason."

It was dumb, stupid, a game lost to all its players. Whatever had come undone in the man, Blue knew the playacting was the beginning of murder.

It was this one killed Mrs. Miller. Had to be. Blue kept his eyes open and unseeing and paid no attention. The big man lost interest and dropped Blue like a gutted hog.

Noises came, and even the distracted big man heard them. The killer spun around, knife raised, eyes hunting for the pursuit. Blue propelled himself into the big man's back, bowling them both through the doorway and out into the hall. The big man hit on his knees, knife still in his hand. The blade twisted in the big fist, and the man howled. The cut was small, but its indignity was uncountable.

The man came up; Blue clung to his back. He wrapped his arms around the wide throat and dug his hands into the windpipe. The howl became a scream, and Blue tore at the leathery skin.

The knife flashed over the big man's shoulder and stabbed at Blue, tearing a piece from his ear, cutting into his torn shoulder. Blue grabbed and clawed, blinded to anything but the big man's death.

A man jumped the last step, black hair flying. A second man followed. The first man drove straight at the beast Blue was riding. The big man saw his new enemy and roared out his hatred. Then Buckminster slammed himself backward, to get rid of the nuisance on his back and prepare for the next battle.

Blue's head cracked on the wall, but his fingers did not let go. Stunned, he held on to Buckminster's neck.

When Buckminster grabbed at Blue with both hands, Peter Charley's long knife slid easily into the unguarded belly and twisted itself home.

Buckminster stood dead on his feet. Peter Charley released Blue's hands from the dead man's neck. Then the huge body folded, the knees gave way, and the hands unclenched. But the eyes stayed open, and when the Indian rolled the immense body over, to retrieve his knife and to know the monster was dead, those eyes stared up at him in blind innocence.

TWENTY-ONE

THE WALL WAS strong, which he needed because his knees were shaking, and he wasn't sure he could stand up by himself. The shapes in front of him sorted out to be two people, then three. Then he could no longer count their numbers.

But he knew Peter Charley stood on one side of him and talked, while the breed kid, Diaz, held up the other side. Blue was grateful for the help.

"Owe you something, Peter Charley." Those were all the words he could spit out. The Indian nodded, dark eyes calm. Then the face split, and the white teeth shaped a grin. The Indian spoke, and Blue knew for certain he was alive. "You damned right, white man. That one, he's no brown bear; he's a damned grizzly killed before."

Peter Charley touched the flank of the corpse on the floor, and Blue shuddered at its size. "How's the girl, Peter Charley?"

He felt the Indian wince. There wasn't time for an answer. Blue could make out Martin Smith coming from the small bedroom. It was easy for him, the stooped shoulders, the slow walk, the manner of the man even in the heart of disaster. Smith came directly into Blue's sight and stood there. Peter Charley melted away, and even Diaz had the sense to get going.

"My daughter is physically fine, Mr. Mitchell. But you, you will have to explain . . . what the hell happened." The

182

fine manners of the boss slipped, and Blue felt a strange sympathy for the man. As if the day had worn off all the gloss and polish. "Peter Charley says you think it's this man who killed Mrs. Miller. Most likely he killed Longacre, too." When Blue started at the news, Smith looked at him, his face grim.

"You didn't now that, did you? Longacre was killed, neck broken. You can see . . . Flora's in there babbling, and I thought he got to her. . . . What happened, Blue? I thought it was shock."

Smith stopped. There were too many people crowding in the hallway, too many ears ready to listen. But Blue knew how to answer without giving details. "It's all right. Flora and me, we talked some. I thanked her for planning to take care of me. But it's over, I can see now, most things at least. Told her it weren't needed, what she was thinking on." He waved an arm and it felt like a hundredweight hanging off his shoulder. "How is she? The son didn't touch her, I don't think. Can't rightly remember, but it was us tangling, and I don't think he laid a hand on her."

Martin Smith answered quietly. "She's scared, badly scared. Like a baby. But she's not hurt, not physically."

Blue couldn't quite see Smith's features, but he could hear the doubt, the question. He wanted to set matters right. "She's a good one, Mr. Smith. Rides like a man. She's tougher than you think. Maybe you been seeing her still a baby, but she's grown up. A pretty girl. I ain't never been nice enough for a girl like that."

Martin Smith stared openly at the man propped up against the wall. He forgot about the crowd and his earlier concerns. This man knew a side of his daughter closed off to him.

As he stared, he thought over the words spoken to him and digested their contents. And continued to take the measure of the man who spoke them. The wild eyes were clearing, the blond hair was streaked with blood and dirt, the cut above the temple was healed. The hands hung motionless, their talents and skills unseen. Like the man himself, until he went to work there was no full measure of what he could do.

A corpse lay on the floor, drained of life and deflated, less than what it had once been as a man. A man judged harmless and then discarded, a man misjudged by his fellow man.

Blue Mitchell was more than good enough for his daughter. Yet Smith could not help but feel relief when the unspoken offer was rejected. She was still a child after all; she still needed growing.

A voice rose in a wail from the small bedroom, and Martin Smith reacted quickly. His daughter needed him. He nodded once at Blue and went about his business.

Blue was grateful to see the stiff-necked man leave. Let him take care of his child, let him leave Blue alone.

"Hey, Indian. Give me a few hours rest, and I'll be ready to ride. You got any place you ain't been to yet that needs seeing, I'll tag along, could do with the company." Then Blue sagged gracelessly, and Peter Charley caught him before he fell.

TWENTY-TWO

THE BROWN GELDING shied from a prairie dog chittering at it, and Blue laughed. He couldn't help himself. The day was perfect, bright sun, trees offering up a thousand leaves turned fall color. The ground was pure dirt, fresh manure, covered with tracks and grasses and the small paths of busy animals. Even stones colored red and yellow sparkled in the light.

And he could see every bit of the world, every miserable stone out to lame his horse, every rustling leaf ready to spook the black pony walking alongside. He could do more than smell the water in the Cimarron. He could count the ripples and throw a stone to the other side.

He could see it all, and he had good company with him, company that knew to keep still and let a man see the world around him, take each breath and sight and sound for the gifts they were.

Blue glanced over at the black pony and the Indian. He grinned, shoved back his hat, and let go of the brown's mouth. The horse jumped, and the black flattened down to run. They were headed south, away from another cold winter, toward a man named Ruben Martinez, who thought he owned the fastest race horse in the small valley.

The sorrel packhorse could catch up later.

ABOUT THE AUTHOR

William A. Luckey lives in Santa Fe, New Mexico. His previous Westerns include *The Death of Joe Gilead*, *Long Ride to Nowhere*, and *Bad Company*.